Sh ɔ
Keep Her Warm

a steamy standalone Regency romance

Sandra Sookoo

New Independence Books

SHE'S GOT A DUKE TO KEEP HER WARM © 2022 by Sandra Sookoo
Published by New Independence Books

ISBN- 9798360210818

Contact Information:
sandrasookoo@yahoo.com
newindependencebooks@gmail.com
Visit me at www.sandrasookoo.com

Book Cover Design Forever After Romance Designs

Publishing History:
First   Print   Edition,   2022

Dear Readers,

What is Christmas without a little bit of spice and heat? In this holiday romance, I've pulled out ALL the stops with a bunch of popular tropes some of you have requested: one room at the inn, snowbound, one bed, young lady lands a duke, widower and brooding hero... you get the picture. Sometimes it's just fun to do all of that.

I hope you enjoy this couple as well as the book. Writing Christmas romances is my jam, and as long as you keep requesting them, I'll keep writing them!

Happy reading! And I wish you the warmest of holidays this year.

Sandra

Dedication

To Jessica Downing. Thank you for your support and enthusiasm about my books. I am so glad you enjoy the escape into my stories. You keep buying them and I'll keep writing them!

Blurb

A lady's companion with no prospects. A duke who has turned his back on romance. A wild snowstorm that leaves them both stranded. It'll be a holiday neither of them will forget.

Resigning herself to becoming a companion to an elderly peeress is Miss Hope Marie Atwater's last chance for a decent life. Though she's unwanted, undesired, and unloved at five and twenty, being on the shelf hasn't completely stolen her spirit. Her one wish at Christmastide is to stumble upon a man who will look past her drab life's circumstances to the spirited woman beneath, but that would take a miracle.

Christmastide only brings maudlin memories he'd rather forget to Brook Gerard Clevenger, Duke of Denton. He wants to bury himself at his country estate, for the thought of merrymaking reminds him of all he's lost. A widower of three years, he's not looking for another romance; one was enough, and the pain will last a lifetime despite the fact he might welcome companionship or the chance for a stolen kiss.

Travelling respectively through north Derbyshire — one coming, one going — misfortune is their lot. A fierce winter storm blows in and strands them at a posting inn where the situation isn't ideal. During a meeting in the courtyard, a common denominator takes them by surprise. As Christmastide nears, the class divide disappears, and the desire simmering between them explodes into something undeniably heated and intense. With three nights until Christmas, the wonder of romance might just be the gift they both need.

Chapter One

December 21, 1810
North of Dronfield
Derbyshire, England

Will this trip ever end?
Miss Hope Atwater tamped on the urge to sigh. Again. She'd done much of that in the last hour and it hadn't helped move the post chaise any faster toward her ultimate destination of Swanson Cottage near the town of Sheffield in Yorkshire. Besides, there were multiple stops between here and there, and at least another day of travel, perhaps more depending on the weather.

The sky was filling with swollen, angry gray clouds that portended more snow. The trip had already been delayed due to snow for three days, which meant the journey that should have taken only four had been extended into a week, and there was no way of knowing how much longer she would need to remain on the dreadful, rutted roads or in the horribly crowded post chaise.

Passengers were picked up or let out along the way, and one never knew who one would be seated next to them in the tight, cramped quarters. Currently, she was squashed between a portly man who had apparently decided bathing with any sort of regularity wasn't for him and a matronly older woman who, each time she nodded off, laid her head — as well as her tilting wig fashionable during the last decade — on Hope's shoulder. And that wig was an odiferous offense.

No amount of sniffing her handkerchief that had been dabbed with her favorite violet perfume could save her nose from the dual assaults.

Across the narrow aisle sat a middle-aged woman who held herself composed and aloof. Perhaps she was a spinster either traveling for a governess position or taking a holiday from the same. There were also two men of indeterminate age, both reading copies of *The Times*, no doubt in the hopes that the other passengers would not engage them in conversation. From the cut of their suits and the quality of the cloth and stitching, they were certainly in a class above the others, but not well-heeled enough that they could secure private transportation. Brothers? Cousins? Father and son? Lovers? Friends? The thoughts on their relationship were endless, and

Hope would entertain herself for an hour or so in putting together stories for them. It was how she'd learned to fill her time whenever she was bored or frightened over her future prospects. Even now, there was a small notebook and pencil in her reticule so she could scribble down some words, which she would then transfer to a current manuscript at a later time.

Honestly, it was the only way she could be certain to give someone a happy ending. There were times when she envied the characters she wrote about.

Because there wasn't a happy ending in the offing for her own life.

Which put her thoughts back on her own circumstances. Three years before, her whole life had been upended, for there had been a horrendous fire at her father's manor house in Hertfordshire. Since it happened during the night somewhere in the kitchens, no one had been aware until it had been too late. The only reason Hope was alive today was due to the fact that a footman had burst into her bedchamber. He'd pulled her and her maid out of the house to safety, but when he'd gone back in to look for her parents, he'd perished due to the smoke. Her parents had never made it outside. Neither had most of the staff.

And that fire had left her scarred both mentally and physically. To say nothing of the fact that it had left her alone at two and twenty.

She'd had no recourse but to take a post chaise down to London and throw herself onto her uncle's doorstep, for with her father dead, his younger brother was the new Baronet Atwater.

He and his wife had taken her in, but they hadn't been happy about it, for they already had two children a handful of years her junior. They'd granted her a Season—after her year of mourning had expired—in the hopes to marry her off. She hadn't managed to attract a titled gentleman, but a lovely lieutenant in the military had asked for her hand. Of course, she'd been highly encouraged to accept the suit, for that meant she'd be off her uncle's hands.

She had but directly following that momentous occasion, he'd received orders to return to his regiment. Because she'd assumed she'd been in love, she'd willingly followed him into scandal one night shortly before his departure. It had been her intention to grant her new fiancé the greatest intimacy, but once she'd pleasured his shaft and they'd undressed, the man had taken one look at her fire-ravaged and scarred skin and had claimed he needed to leave. That had been heartbreaking, but when he'd begged off the engagement in a letter after he'd left London, her confidence and trust had been shattered.

Obviously, she was too damaged and ugly to attract a man. It taken a long time to move past that incident, wherein she'd languished around London, neither wishing to move through society as much as she should nor making an effort to find friends. Her uncle hadn't been pleased. Eventually, when she'd turned five and twenty in the spring of this year, he'd advised her to take a companion position for an elderly peeress, so her failure wouldn't ruin his children's chances.

With another sigh, this one of desolation, Hope tried to squirm into a more comfortable position between her seat mates, and once more moved the woman's head off her shoulder. The letter of introduction as well as the one of acceptance from the dowager Lady Lesterfield rested in her reticule next to her notebook. That lady was the daughter of a duke and had married a marquess in her heyday, but she'd never had children, and from all accounts, she had aged into a crotchety, overly critical, sourpuss of a woman.

And now she needed a companion… or rather a new one, for there had already been an impressive string of women who had preceded Hope.

Only God knew how long her position would last before it was terminated, or she gave notice. For the time being, this is what her life had become. However, the dowager's nephew had been scheduled to meet her and then escort her for the rest of the journey, but he hadn't made an appearance, so she'd been forced to continue by herself.

She frowned out the window where the snow had finally begun to fly, and at a rather fast clip. *Oh, please let us not become stranded.* That would just add insult to injury. *Will this trip ever end?* The thought certainly bore repeating.

When she attempted to make eye contact with the woman across the narrow aisle, she was rebuffed. Neither did the men with the newspapers look her way. Even though the coach's interior was crowded, it seemed an extremely lonely place.

And quite frankly, she had grown tired of being alone.

As the wind increased and began to howl, the hiss of snow against the window glass sent a shiver down her spine. Winter, in general, wasn't one of her favorite seasons, but she would have gladly welcomed it if she wasn't currently sitting in a coach slowly trundling northward, which would put her right in the center of more of the same. The northern climes always ran the risk of having more snow than the London area.

Another hour passed wherein her patience had all but evaporated, for being stuck between her bench mates had grown intolerable. Then the inevitable happened. The unmistakable snap of wood splintering echoed in the air, quickly followed by an ominous tilting of the vehicle. She was smashed against the body of the woman next to her and then given the ultimate indignity of being groped by the portly man as his body layered into hers by the situation.

This is outside of enough!

With a frustrated huff, Hope wriggled out from between the other two people and then unceremoniously tumbled to the tilting floor, slid down, and landed on her bottom against the door. At that moment, one of the drivers swung open that panel. She spilled out of the chaise in a tangle of limbs and skirting to land at his feet, staring up at the white-painted world around her.

"Begging your pardon, miss," the man said as he put a gloved hand beneath her upper arm and hauled her into a standing position without ceremony. "Seems we've broken a wheel out here. Can't see the ruts in the road with all this snow."

Another shiver racked her shoulders as she regained her footing and moved a few steps away from the leaning chaise. "Is it repairable?" The other driver had jumped down from the box and came around to assess the situation.

He was the one who answered. "Sure, we can repair it, but it'll take time. Folly to do so in this storm. Will only be able to travel another mile or so before we're forced to stop anyway."

As a few other people came out of the chaise, Hope rubbed her hands up and down her arms. The woolen pelisse in a maroon color she'd worn might have been lined with a thin layer of rabbit fur, but with the wind and the exuberant snow, the temperature was rapidly declining. Additionally, the woolen muslin skirts weren't heavy enough to keep her legs warm.

Drat. I should have worn a second petticoat. Of course, how was she to know weather conditions would deteriorate?

"I assume you will repair the wheel so we can continue on, then?" the overweight man who'd sat beside her asked. His top hat kept lifting off his balding head due to the wind.

"We will change out the wheel, of course." The second driver looked him up and down with narrowed eyes. "But we won't continue unless you want to help guide the horses through the weather. It's not going to improve anytime soon."

Before the man could respond, the first driver nodded. "Don't want to risk the animals or the wheels on a road we can't see. Or run the risk of being stuck in a drift."

One of the men who'd been reading the newspaper scoffed. "What are we to do, then? We're nowhere close to where we should have stopped for the night, and we do have a schedule to keep."

It took all of Hope's willpower to not roll her eyes skyward.

But the second driver shook his head. "There is a posting inn about a half mile up the road called The Brown Hare. Can't say if there are rooms available at this late date."

The portly man shook his head. "You expect us to walk all that way? And what of our luggage?"

Hope bounced her gaze between the men as best she could with the flying snow. "It is only a half mile. Be grateful for that."

One of the drivers nodded. "Mayhap some of the stable hands at the inn will help in hauling the luggage. Could be stranded a good while if the weather keeps up."

"And pray brigands don't come by to rifle through our trunks?"

This time, Hope *did* roll her eyes. "Do you truly think bandits and thieves will be about on the roads in this storm?"

While the overweight man stewed, the drivers snickered. "What do you know about it, miss?"

She blinked snowflakes from her lashes. "I know that if we continue to stand around, we'll be covered in snow, and I would rather not freeze." Already, the snow on the ground reached the ankles of her half boots. "And let us pray there are no drifts in our path."

The second driver grinned. "You should listen to her. The storm will probably dig in for a while." As he spoke, the remaining travelers came out of the coach. "Best get started." He pointed north. "Follow the road as best you can. The inn rests a bit back from the thoroughfare, but you can't miss it."

"What if we do?" one of the gentlemen asked with a dubious expression.

The first driver shrugged, but there was an unrepentant grin on his face. "You'll surely freeze."

Hope grasped the strings of her reticule tighter. "Thank you both for ensuring we reached this far without incident. I look forward to resuming our travels." And if the storm did indeed delay the trip, it meant a couple more days of free time before she took up the reins of companion.

"Truly our pleasure, miss." The second driver winked. "Good fortune to you."

"Thank you." She swept her gaze around at her assembled fellow passengers. "You may stand about and continue debating, but I am heading out for the inn." When no one made inroads into departing with her, she shrugged, waved to the drivers, bent her shoulders into the wind, and set out to follow the road while she could still see it. Teatime had come and gone, but with the wind, the rapidly falling snow, and the dark gray skies, it was rather darker earlier than it should have been.

By the time the outlines of the roof came into view, Hope's feet were frozen. Snow had caked upon her shoulders as well as her bonnet. Her ears smarted from the cold. Flakes of snow stuck to her eyelashes and those eyes streamed from the chilly wind. To say nothing of how frigid her fingers were, for the thin kid did nothing to insulate her digits from the weather.

As she stumbled off what she assumed was still the road and toward the innyard, she realized the coins that rested at the bottom of her reticule were probably not enough to cover the expense of a bed, let alone a whole room. Even if she had to share. She was too cold to shiver with revulsion, for if she were forced to split a bed with people the likes of which she'd shared a post chaise with, she would vastly prefer to sleep on the floor.

Halfway across the innyard, two matched dappled gray mares bore down on her. Snow covered the driver's hat and the muffler wrapped around his face, so she couldn't blame him for not being able to see her. Regardless, she stood rooted to the snowy ground, too exhausted to dart away, and stared with her heart in her throat as the horses came ever closer.

At the last second, the driver pulled the animals under control, but not before she was knocked once more to her bottom, so close that the whites of the horses' eyes were visible directly above her and the stream of their breath warmed the side of her face.

"Damn and blast!" Or at least that's what she assumed the driver said, for she couldn't see his lips. "You fool woman! Could have been killed!"

Hope blinked. Her chest was tight with shock as well as fright while the horses stamped with impatience. She crawled out from beneath the first one but didn't have the strength to stand just yet. Instead, she stared at the snow-covered ground and tried to catch her breath. Then a pair of shiny black Hessians appeared in her line of vision. Obviously, their owner hadn't had to tramp across the countryside for the last hour. Then she drew her gaze up, but the man's legs were mostly hidden by a black greatcoat. Her perusal stopped, for he extended a hand that was encased in a brown kid glove.

"I apologize for the accident. It is rather treacherous out here just now."

Well, at least the man had manners. It was more than she could say for her fellow passengers. "It has been a long time since I've seen such a winter." She slipped her fingers into his palm, and easily he lifted her into a standing position. "Thank you." As she peered upward into the man's face, the amusement and concern dancing in his blue eyes held her captive. A glimpse of blond hair was visible beneath the brim of his beaver felt top hat.

"Think nothing of it." He didn't release her hand, and she rather liked the firm grip of his fingers. "Are you staying at The Brown Hare?"

"I am hoping to, if it is not too expensive for the coin in my possession." *Well, drat.* She shouldn't have told him that lest he now think her a beggar. A shiver raced down her spine; it was quite cold, made even more so by her snow-damp clothing. "The post chaise I'd traveled on broke a wheel and is stranded on the road due to the weather. It was an unforeseen misfortune."

"That is largely why I am here. The snow has thwarted by own travel plans." The well-modulated baritone voice sent a different sort of shiver through her insides.

She glanced past his broad shoulders to the front door of the charming and unassuming inn. The sign hanging above the door depicted a painting of a brown rabbit. "Do you think it's full up?" To her chagrin, her teeth chattered.

"I would have no idea, but perhaps we should make our way inside. I can feel you shivering." He half-turned back toward his coach. "Gerald, I'm going into the inn. Get yourself into the stables and dried out in the kitchens."

"Of course, my lord."

Then he focused his attention back on her. A frown tugged the corners of his mouth downward. "Standing here talking of nothing is not helping, Miss…?"

"Atwater. Miss Hope Atwater." She would have shrugged but the gesture turned into a large shiver instead. "It's only natural since I have been walking for an hour. At this point, I rather doubt I'll ever feel warm again." Once more she looked into his face. Though slight surprise had jumped into his eyes, he seemed slightly familiar.

He leaned his head toward hers while at the same time urging her through the snow toward the door. "I'm the Duke of Denton."

Oh, dear heavens! "A pleasure to finally make your acquaintance, Your Grace." She should curtsy, but honestly, she was too tired and cold, and she didn't wish to disturb his hand tucked over hers that rested on his sleeve. "Your title sounded familiar to me, and I have seen you about London a few times." The duke was considered one of the best catches of the *ton*, even if he was a widower a bit over two years.

"Indeed. Truth to tell, I'd rather be back in London instead of out here, but at least this trip has excused me from having to do the social circuit this Christmastide." Then he ushered her inside, and blessed warmth immediately surrounded her. All thoughts racing through her head evaporated in her quest to seek out more of that warmth. "You must be near frozen."

"I am." It was all too lovely to have someone look after her well-being, and to be in the company of a duke, to boot! The situation would have tickled her, but she was much too cold to give into her sense of humor.

"Come." The man escorted her into the large common room with its smoky beams across the ceiling and dark, heavy furniture. At a large hearth, he ushered her into a nearby straight-backed wooden chair. "Sit here and thaw. I shall see to procuring a couple of rooms for the night."

Immediately, she shook her head. "Oh, I couldn't allow you to do that, Your Grace. I am perfectly capable of—"

"My driver nearly ran you over. I owe you at least this." A tiny smile curved his mouth. "Warm yourself. I shall return shortly."

With a sigh, Hope sank onto the chair and turned her body closer to the gloriously crackling fire. For the moment, she wouldn't press her case. It wasn't her lot to accept charity. Perhaps her spirit would rally once she had the full use of her frozen extremities.

Chapter Two

Brook Clevenger—the 6th Duke of Denton—frowned as he made his way through the common room that grew more crowded with every passing moment. The woman he'd escorted into the posting inn was the same woman he had been scheduled to meet yesterday at a different inn, the woman he'd been tasked in escorting into Yorkshire as his aunt's companion.

The fact she hadn't lingered in an effort to wait for him at the meeting place both amused and disconcerted him. When he'd received a letter from his aunt earlier in the month asking him to retrieve and then escort the new companion, it wasn't that out of the ordinary, for the dowager had gone through at least eight unfortunate souls in that position during the past two years. What he *had* objected to was leaving his comfortable chair in front of his cheerful fire in his London townhouse, for the Christmastide season didn't lend itself well to his wish to remain alone and shrouded with memories.

Yet, he would never hear the end of it if he'd declined, so here he was. No doubt ten minutes away from being stranded at a godforsaken inn in the middle of nowhere due to a snowstorm no one had anticipated being this bad.

With a glance at Miss Atwater—who had removed her gloves and had stretched her hands out toward the fire in the hearth—he sighed. He had no doubts his aunt would completely run that young woman off in less than three months. Usually, the women who applied for the position of her companions were made of sterner stuff and spinsters well on the shelf—dour if he were truthful—all things Miss Atwater was not.

Though now the question of how she'd come to be in this position at all bedeviled him.

"May I help you?"

The sound of a man's voice wrenched Brook from his thoughts. With another frown, he rested his gaze on the clerk behind the polished counter. The Brown Hare Inn might be a touch cozy and out of the way, but it was clean and tidy, and someone had polished the brass fixtures in the room with care.

"I would like to request two private rooms, if you please."

"Unfortunately, we only have one private room left, or you are welcome to share a bed in one of our other rooms. So far there are only two occupants of each bed. Plenty of room."

"Ah." With another glance at Miss Atwater, he gave the full of his attention to the clerk. The young woman was much too delicate—and clean—to be forced into sharing a room as well as a bed with God only knew who else. And why the devil didn't she have a maid accompanying her? She had been much too well spoken not to be part of the *ton*, and she hinted as much when she'd said she'd seen him in society. He hadn't a blessed clue who she was and couldn't place the name. "Then I shall gladly pay for your last private room."

"For just you?"

This decision would affect both his future and Miss Atwater's if word were to get back to London, but surely there was no reason for that to happen. Reminding himself he was doing this to protect her from worse things—though he had absolutely no reason for it—he shook his head. "No. My wife is with me." Perhaps this was his way of apologizing for the shrew his aunt would be, and the life Miss Atwater would face as the woman's companion.

"I see." Though there was nothing in the other man's face to indicate Brook lied, muscles still knotted in his belly. It had been a bit over two years since he'd used that moniker, and should never have, for his own wife had died quite horrifically; he didn't wish to be reminded of that, but there was nothing for it. "What is your name?"

What, indeed? He couldn't very well give his real name or title. That would be folly and near societal suicide. "Mr. Gerard and my wife, Hope. We are, uh, newlyweds." That would explain any awkwardness between them seeing as how they were strangers. Remarkably, his voice remained calm and even. It was his middle name, and hardly anyone knew it. Though he'd not made it a habit of dissembling, the lie tripped easily off his tongue. "We are, uh, traveling to see family for the Christmastide season." That was a half-truth also. He and Miss Atwater *were* traveling to family, but there would be no celebrations involved.

"Very good, Mr. Gerard." The clerk printed the name into a larger ledger book resting on the countertop. "How many days will you need the room?"

"I had hoped just for tonight." But a glance outside showed nothing but the heavy, swirling snow. More of the same blew into the common room when the door opened to admit two men in greatcoats as well as a portly gentleman. "Though, I'll wager this storm won't clear out any time soon. Why don't I keep it through Christmas and then we can reevaluate the likelihood of extending a stay?"

"Of course, Mr. Gerard." The sound of the quill scratching over the ledger paper reached

Brook's ears. "The Brown Hare charges three shillings a night for a private room. Dinner is not included and must be paid for separately."

Brook's eyebrows rose. "That is quite a steep price. One can rent a room in London for seven shillings a *week*." The expense was staggering, so it was good he would enter into this charade, for Miss Atwater probably didn't have enough coin in her possession to pay for any sort of lodging.

"It's the cost of demand, Mr. Gerard. The winter is sometimes lean, but we can counter our potential losses when storms hit." The clerk shrugged. "If you turn down the room, there are others who will gladly snap it up. You and your wife can then share a room and bed, or you can stay in the stables."

It would seem one didn't need to be on the road to be a victim of highway robbery, but business was indeed business. "Fine." He dug into a pocket of his greatcoat and withdrew a small leather pouch. From there, he took out the required coins plus an additional guinea, which he plunked upon the counter. "I will let the room for five nights, with the caveat you will offer it back to me at the end of the term before letting it to someone else. The extra is to see to our meals as well as house my coach, look after my horse, and my driver."

"Very good, Mr. Gerard." The coins disappeared into a strongbox beneath the counter. Then he dropped a brass key into Brook's palm. "Room seven. Second floor left side. End of the corridor. It overlooks the woods and will provide enough privacy for you."

"Thank you." He tucked the key into his waistcoat pocket. "Is there a private dining room available for dinner tonight? If so, I would like to reserve one." Obviously too late for tea, the next chance to put anything worthwhile in his belly was the evening meal. Thank goodness country hours were earlier than what he usually kept in London.

"Of course, Mr. Gerard." The clerk flipped to another page and drew a long finger down a column of numbers. "There is one left during our six o'clock hour. In future, might I suggest reserving earlier? We only have four in circulation, and the inn is quite full."

Brook clenched his teeth. "Since I only just arrived and didn't know of the inn's existence until now, I couldn't have made a reservation earlier, could I?" Remaining polite only went so far when there was a lack of commonsense at play.

"Now you know for future reference." A slight curl flashed on the man's upper lip.

"Yes, so I do." It would give him great pleasure to reveal his true identity to this man who thought himself superior. "Then perhaps this will also serve as notice that I need the same private dining room for each night of my stay."

If Miss Atwater didn't go along with his insane plan, he would need some place to retreat to in order to escape her wrath.

"I will mark you down, Mr. Gerard." Again, the pen nub scratched along the paper.

"Thank you."

"You, there, chap," said the overweight man who now stood directly behind Brook. The fellow even dared to tap him on the shoulder. "If you've concluded your business, move aside. We all need rooms."

"So you do." And good luck to whomever had to bed down with that rotund bit of rudeness. "Pardon me." He stepped around the man with a nod to the other two men. From the way their outer things were snow covered, he assumed this trio had ridden in the post chaise with Miss Atwater. None of them gave him the respect due a duke, but then, no one aside from his driver and Miss Atwater knew that truth.

Before he revealed his plans to the young lady, he took a tour about the room. Much of a duke's influence was making connections and allies, and that required a man to either be congenial or intimidating. There was no harm in finding out who he would share the inn with over the foreseeable future. In less than twenty minutes, he'd met a magistrate traveling home to his empty cottage, a vicar who was trying to reach his sister before she gave birth, a prize fighter returning to London after having won a sizable purse at a bout, a German princess going to a friend's holdings in the north to spend the holiday season, a merchant and his wife who wished to spend their anniversary in London as a treat, a young widow with a small daughter who was traveling to Hertsfordshire to live with her deceased husband's parents, two brothers who were both in their twenties apparently fleeing London with scandal on their heels, and a young couple hoping to elope to Gretna Green.

That was by no means the entirety of the inn's clientele, but it was enough to put him at ease. He'd of course introduced himself as Mr. Gerard enroute to a holiday with his new bride. There was no threat from any of these folks, and it was enough of a mix that conversation during forced proximity would prove interesting and enlightening. Perhaps a game of cards would be in the offing at some point.

By the time he joined his wife of convenience by the fire, he'd shed his outer things and laid them on a small, round table at his elbow. "I have managed to secure lodging for the next handful of nights."

"Oh?" She glanced at him, and there was so much relief and gratitude in her doe brown eyes that he couldn't look away. His wife had had brown eyes, but while Deborah's had been a rich brandy hue, Miss Atwater's were a deeper brown. A jagged spear of grief went through his chest. Even after two years and four months, that grief still caught him at the most unexpected times. "How much do I owe you?" When she took her reticule into her lap and began rooting through it, he held up a hand.

"Nothing. I have absorbed the cost, but for the sake of both our reputations and ease of said lodging, there are a couple of things you'll need to know." What sort of woman was she? Would she fall into hysterics once he told her what would happen? Would she demand that he cancel the room?

"What do you mean?" She clutched her fingers tightly in her lap.

Brook rubbed a hand along the side of his face. With a sigh, he held her gaze. "There were no regular rooms available unless you wished to share a bed with two other people. More so now, I'll wager. So, I inquired about private rooms."

"And?"

"I went ahead and took the room." Then he lowered his voice and leaned toward her, for the common room was becoming more crowded than it was before. "However, we must pretend we are a couple newly wed." When her pink-hued lips parted and shock flitted through her eyes, he nodded. "Out of necessity, I have told the clerk of this inn that you are my wife and that we are Mr. and Mrs. Gerrard."

"Why would you lie and not tell them you are a duke?" Her voice was little more than a whisper.

Instead of answering immediately, he moved his chair a bit closer to her. "Take a glance about the room, Miss Atwater," he said in an equally low tone. "Did you want to risk sharing a room—and a bed—with some of these people?" Though there were perfectly lovely travelers in the room, there were also some unsavory types. It would be wise for everyone to lock their doors in the night.

When her gaze landed on the portly man who had obviously just been given the news he'd have to bed down with others, she shuddered. "I sat next to that man for a day on my journey."

"Then you agree to participate in my bit of fiction?" One of his eyebrows rose in question. "No one here besides me knows of your real identity."

"Are you certain you aren't doing this to protect your *own* reputation?" Annoyance caused her voice to rise, but she quickly modulated her tone. "Why would you do this for a woman so beneath your station? I am nothing to you."

Well, at least she had spirit. That would ensure their stay wouldn't be dull. "Of course I'm protecting my reputation. Any man in my position would, but I am also protecting yours. As to why?" That he couldn't explain. Perhaps he'd been away from society for too long and out of the company of a woman for the same, or perhaps he'd merely wanted to play the hero. "You are too much a lady to mingle with the clientele in such an intimate fashion."

She snorted. "*Lady* is rather pushing my pedigree."

"Why would you say that?" Perhaps she would give him a bit of her history.

"My father was a baronet. Therefore, I am not a lady, and neither was he a peer. My grip on the *ton* at large is tenuous at best." Miss Atwater narrowed her eyes on him. "Most likely you and I would never have met while in London. We don't move in the same social circles, and I in none of them since my father died."

"I am sorry for your loss."

"Thank you. So am I, even more so during this time of year." She lapsed into silence and then tugged on the maroon ribbon beneath her chin. Once she removed her bonnet and set it in her lap, she sighed. "Life hasn't been quite the same since my parents died."

"I empathize with you on that." Maudlin feelings welled into his chest. His own journey through life had been marked by more deaths than he cared to remember. "Grief doesn't go away or fade as time goes on like people often say when offering counsel."

"No." She shook head. In the firelight, strands of caramel glimmered in her brown hair, and he suddenly wished those tresses weren't held back in a tight, neat bun. "Grief is a funny thing. It becomes part of you, and you make room for it. The heart might heal but grief will always be a part of everything you are."

"Indeed." As Brook studied his companion of the moment, it struck him that she was a delicate slip of a young woman. The pelisse hid her body and made her as generic as any other female in the common room, but her fingers were slim and feminine. With a heart-shaped face and features that could only be described as pixyish, she had the look of always either knowing a secret or getting ready to do mischief. "There are other times when I fully believe the person suffering through grief doesn't wish that pain to fade, for fear that it might take the memories with it."

He'd certainly felt that way over the years. Though some memories were still as poignant as the day they were made, others had faded with time. No longer could he see a person's face or features clearly in his mind. Though he could still hear scraps of laughter or feel the touch of a hand, other aspects slipped further away as the years went on.

That was his biggest fear since losing his wife. He didn't want to forget, yet each remembrance left him with the same pain he'd had since losing her so suddenly.

"Agreed." Miss Atwater nodded. "Then there are other memories that make a person mourn for things never realized, even when the people involved are still very much alive." A trace of bitterness went through her voice. Shadows reflected in her eyes. Then she shrugged. "Time is either a balm or a curse, I suppose. It merely depends on one's mood."

What the devil had she seen over the course of her young life to give her such sage advice? Curiosity reigned, but he wouldn't ask her here where they ran the risk of being overheard. Before he could say anything else, the loud rumble of her stomach broke the silence brewing between them.

Her gaze flew to his. A blush infused her cheeks, and the added color gave life to her pale face. "Do pardon me. It has been some time since I've last eaten."

"Then you are fortunate. I have reserved a private dining room for our dinner at six o'clock." Hoping to cajole a smile from her, Brook flashed a grin. "We won't need to wait much longer before we're able to tuck into a meal."

"That sounds lovely. I hope the inn employs a decent cook." She laid a hand on his arm. Immediately warmth tingled up to his elbow. It had been a long time since he'd had such close interaction with a woman to whom he wasn't related. "And thank you again for looking after me even though there wasn't a need." The soulful gratitude shining in those eyes was all the thanks he required, and if he wasn't careful, he'd fall right into those pools. "It has been ages since anyone has cared enough to do that."

"I am happy to do it." His wife had been the one to remind him that he had a responsibility to look after anyone down on their luck he came across. Privilege meant helping others, and so he had done so with aplomb since he'd lost her, but there was something about Miss Atwater that had excitement buzzing at the base of his spine, and that troubled him.

Perhaps it had been a nodcock idea to share a room. *She is not for you, Denton. Haven't you already promised yourself you would never again get close to a woman?* Indeed, he had, and that reasoning had worked until his horse had nearly trampled this one and he'd plucked her out of the snow.

But he was certain their stay at The Brown Hare Inn would pass without incident. The mild temptation she represented would pass, and his interest would fade. It's what had happened since he'd come out of mourning. After everything, he was a gentleman, and his only task was in delivering her to his aunt.

So why, then, hadn't he mentioned that little tidbit to her when he'd had the chance?

Chapter Three

❖━━━━━❖━❖━━━━━❖

Muscles knotted with anxiety in Hope's stomach as she sat down to dinner with the Duke of Denton in one of the private dining rooms at The Brown Hare Inn. Though she was ravenously hungry, she didn't know if she could eat in front of a man so high on the instep. To say nothing of the fact that since she was here with him alone, they were already skirting the bounds of propriety. If this had been London, nearly everyone would be demanding that the duke ask for her hand in marriage due to the taint of her being compromised, yet here, tucked away in a snowbound inn where they were portraying themselves as a wedded couple, everything was far removed from reality.

As they finished with a chicken velvet soup and a member of the staff placed plates of roast beef with creamed potatoes and roasted carrots in front of them, a hunger pang rumbled once more. Perhaps a man's status didn't count when it came to matters of the stomach.

"One would think I hadn't a meal in a week instead of just a day." The duke sliced through his meat, speared that chunk with his fork, and then popped it into his mouth and chewed, apparently happy in the moment.

"There is something about travel that makes a person hungrier, I think." She sampled a forkful of the creamed potatoes. They were decent for a posting inn's offerings, so she settled into making inroads into her meal. The roast beef wasn't as tender as it could be, but it had decent flavor and plenty of gravy, and the carrots hadn't been cooked to complete mush.

Eventually, the mad rush of eating slowed, which made room for conversation. "Where did you come up with Gerard as a surname, especially in haste?" she finally asked, since it was but one question sitting uppermost on her mind.

He took a sip from his glass of red wine. "It is one of my middle names."

"I see." Hope took another bite of the potatoes before declaring defeat with a full stomach. "Do you often go about rescuing young women by pretending to be married?"

"Of course not." The corners of his mouth twitched with the beginnings of a grin that never quite materialized. "This is the first time I have ever put forth this bit of fantasy."

"I don't know whether to be in awe of how your mind works or wary that you've included me in this deception."

"It was either this or survive the gauntlet of luck for however many days we might be stranded at this inn." The budding grin vanished altogether, and shadows clouded his eyes.

Unease pushed down her spine. "Do you think we'll be here for longer than one night?"

"Well, let's see." The duke stood up from his chair and moved to the window. Slightly curious, Hope followed until she stood at his shoulder and peered out at the wooded area. "There has been no respite from the snow since we arrived almost two hours ago. And with that wind, drifting will be an issue soon enough."

"Then the prospect of traveling tomorrow is slim?"

"I'm afraid so." He sounded as glum as she felt. Why, though?

Instead of seeing the snow outside the window glass, she watched his reflection. Now that he didn't have the greatcoat on, she could study his form without impediment. Broad shoulders set off by a jacket of sapphire superfine. An ivory satin waistcoat embroidered with blue and silver swirls drew the eye to his flat abdomen, and the buff-colored breeches tucked into the shiny Hessians fairly begged for her stare.

"That's not exactly how I'd hoped to spend the days leading up to Christmas." Her gaze shifted in the window reflection to herself and the frown she leveled at the glass. At such close proximity, the scent of his shaving soap—sandalwood and citrus—teased her nose. It was both mysterious and familiar. "And it only postpones the inevitable."

The duke turned toward her. Those intense blue eyes were slightly unsettling, as if he were peering into her soul. "Meaning?"

"Meaning I am on my way to Yorkshire to fill a companion post to an elderly peeress. Likely, it is what will become of the remainder of my life."

He snorted. "Well, at least until the peeress succumbs to death."

"Yes, I suppose, but after that, I will simply move on to the next post. That is all there is for me at this point." Hope wandered back to the round wooden table where the detritus of their dinner was growing progressively colder. It was a good idea to keep distance between them, for there was something about the man that had flutters flitting through her lower belly. She had no business finding out why. "I know little to nothing about her other than she is a bit persnickety, but I have no choice." In some dejection, she slipped into the chair she'd recently vacated and frowned at her half-drunk glass of wine.

"What would you say if I told you I already knew who you were?" The duke reseated himself at the table but never took his gaze from hers. "As well as her?"

"I beg your pardon, Your Grace?" Was he making jest of her?

"First of all, please call me Brook but only when we are alone. If you wish to remain somewhat formal, you may also refer to me as Denton." Faint humor shimmered in his eyes that were so blue they reminded her of the lake on her father's country property. "To the general public here at the inn, I am Mr. Gerard."

And she was Mrs. Gerard.

A tingle of excitement shivered down her spine. Perhaps the ruse would prove entertaining. "I rather like the sound of Brook." She gave him a small smile. "You may call me Hope. Now please, explain to me how you knew who I am."

"The dowager Lady Lesterfield is my aunt. She is my father's sister. I was the one tasked with escorting you up to Yorkshire." When he shrugged, his jacket pulled tight over his chest. "Due to the weather, my travels were delayed, and I couldn't meet you yesterday as my aunt had outlined in her letter."

"I'd wondered what had happened, but I had no idea I would be met by a duke." It made the situation better only slightly, and it also assumed he had brought at least some staff with him. So, where were they? "It was happenstance we were both stranded here on the same day."

"Agreed."

"If it was true and there were only a few rooms left, what did you do with your staff?" Her family might not have many servants, but he was a duke. There were always people around someone so close to royalty.

"I like the fact you are intelligent." He lifted his wineglass to his lips, and once more she studied him. Strong aristocratic features, chiseled lips, full blond eyebrows, and a nose that reminded her of similar appendages she'd once seen in Elgin's Marbles. It was true that he was classically handsome, but not overly so. No doubt one only thought so due to the fact he was a duke. "When it became evident the weather wouldn't improve, I ordered them all into the second travelling coach and sent them back to London. There was no need for us all to risk the rigors of wintertime travel, and they might as well spend the holiday in comfort with their own hearths and friends."

That was unexpectedly kind and considerate. "But such a decision left you alone."

This time, a full-blown grin curved his lips, and she stared for it took years from his face. "It is not difficult to dress oneself, Hope." The way he said her name, as if he caressed the word with his lips before releasing it into the air, made her shiver with a need she didn't fully understand. "Neither is it a chore to shave and style my hair without assistance. In fact, I rather looked forward to not having a bevy of servants about me all the time."

It was an interesting way of seeing life through a different point of view. "I'm glad you sent your staff back, for it would have been a miserable experience staying in a strange kitchen or stables."

"Indeed, and I hope they have a better time of it than I did as I continued on, but then the winters are often worse in the north than in the south." When she merely stared at him, for she fell into the trap of watching his mouth as he talked, he continued. "Where is your maid?"

Hope shook herself out of her thoughts. "I don't have one. Not really. There was an upstairs maid, but my aunt and I shared her."

"Ah, and your aunt wasn't about to give her up."

"Exactly, and as you said, it is not difficult to dress oneself." In fact, she had only brought one gown that required any sort of assistance—and one that required assistance—for there was every possibility she wouldn't have need of the others in her position as a companion. Then a new thought occurred. "I do hope the drivers were able to secure help in bringing the luggage to the inn." Otherwise, it would be a long stint of days with just her traveling ensemble to wear.

"I shall check on the progress when we are done here."

She nodded. "Thank you. At least there will be some comforts of home then."

For long moments, he sipped his wine while watching her. "Because I'm curious, I must ask how the devil you thought to be a companion to an elderly peeress. Surely there are other positions you could fill."

What type of positions? Surely, he wasn't as crass as to mean a mistress. Heat went into her cheeks from embarrassment. "When my parents died, I traveled to London to live with my uncle and his wife."

"Ah, and suddenly you were the unwanted, poor relation." There was no judgment or censure in his voice, only understanding.

"Yes." She nodded and dropped her gaze to her plate of half-finished food. "I had a Season which didn't take as we all had hoped and ended to even more disastrous results." Of which she didn't wish to talk about right now. "When it became obvious I wasn't marriageable material, my uncle and his wife weren't pleased with the prospects of another mouth to feed. Neither did they want the stigma of an unlaunched family member to hinder their own children's prospects." That had been the worst aspect of the years spent there—the lack of pride. Would it have been such a bad thing for her uncle to say he was proud of her for surviving what she had and that he would look after her well-being until she could discover what she wanted from life?

"And the only solution was for you to take a paid position somewhere." The sound of his voice had her raising her gaze. Truly it was a delightful rumble.

"Also true. My uncle applied for a few positions on my behalf before your aunt answered the letter."

"Well, she has a reputation for being rather high-spirited and opinionated." Another tiny grin tugged on the corners of his lips. What would a kiss from him feel like?

Immediately, she shoved the inappropriate thought away. "I am spirited as well and have a rather strong backbone. I am hopeful I can counter whatever the lady choses to throw my way."

The light of interest sprang into his eyes. "Well, your name *is* Hope, after all."

Another round of heat went through her cheeks. "There has been little enough of that to go around in my life, but I do remain positive."

"How old are you... Hope?"

Awareness of him skated over her skin, bringing gooseflesh with it. Perhaps it was nothing more than the drafts of cold in the air brought on by the howling wind. "I turned five and twenty a few months ago." Why was that pertinent?

"Ah. I see." He nodded as if the information pleased him. "My aunt hasn't had a companion so young before. I wonder if that will make the difference." A thoughtful expression crossed his face. "Perhaps you will be the one my aunt doesn't manage to either sack or run off."

"Oh." With such a history, her chances of retaining the position lowered by the minute. "I wasn't aware she was… difficult." That made her doubly grateful for the delay in travel.

An unexpected laugh issued from the duke, and it was such a rich, vibrant sound that her lower jaw dropped, and she stared in unabashed wonder at him. "Aunt Cynthia is certainly set in her ways. When she resided in London, she could barely keep servants, for she had a bit of a reputation."

"Was she always like that?"

"No. Not always." Some of his levity faded, and the customary shadows returned to his eyes. "Once her husband died, she changed, as we all do when grief comes to call. I think she rather misses him terribly. And then, when my father—her brother—perished, that only compounded her anguish."

"That is understandable." Hope peered more closely at the duke. Lines furrowed his brow and framed the corners of his eyes. More than anything else, he appeared… tired. Not in a physical sense but in a soul-exhausted way. There were times when she'd thought her uncle had the same look, yet he never spoke about his feelings. "In London, gossip holds you have become a bit of a recluse since your wife died. Is that true?" With the next gust of wind, the candles in the room guttered. There was no doubt it would prove a cold night.

"I suppose it is." The duke drained the last of the wine in his glass. Though he eyed hers, he didn't ask for it. "It has been two years and four months. After she died, I suddenly didn't see the value in mingling amidst the shallow, critical *ton* any longer." He guided a fingertip along the rim of the wine glass, and though he looked at her, she doubted he saw her, for he was temporarily lost to the past. "For the whole of my seven and thirty years, everything I have ever done is to help navigate the waters of society, gain connections, strengthen alliances, fill the coffers, amass wealth and power, or beget an heir." His voice broke on the last word. "And where has it gotten me?" When he shook his head, his gaze came back to the present. "A wife and child in the cold ground, a handful of estates scattered throughout England that I cannot bring myself to visit, and a worn chair in front of my fire in my London townhouse where I spend the bulk of my time because I can no longer bear to visit with my friends."

"Without her, correct?" It was a guess, of course, but gossip also held that the duke had adored his wife. And going by her own parents' example of marriage, losing a spouse must have been a terribly painful endeavor.

"Yes." Brook shot to his feet in order to pace the length of the small dining room. "All of my friends knew me as a happily married man. Many of them are also married. How do I fit into that world now I'm a widower?"

Poor man. "They are still your friends, Your Grace."

Once he turned, he glanced at her with a raised eyebrow. "Brook."

"Right. Brook." Heat went through her cheeks. His presence seemed to fill the room, and she was all too aware of him. "I am certain they wish to support you regardless of your marital state, and undoubtedly they can help you navigate your grief more fully."

Or so she hoped. It was something sorely missing from life in London, where it was frowned upon to talk about one's feelings and emotions, especially if one was part of the *ton*. But to whose detriment? For that matter, why were people taught to keep a stiff upper lip to begin with? Was it merely an English tradition or did the general populace simply not understand how to support others when their distress smacked even the slightest bit of mental disturbance?

"I would rather not try." He resumed pacing. "Besides, it was my wife who adored balls and routs and the like. She was ever the social butterfly, the true face of the title. Without her by my side, I am quite ill at ease."

"That surprises me. I assumed every man who held a dukedom was naturally poised and possessed of self-confidence." This was a fascinating glimpse into the life of someone she would never have met if it weren't for this trip.

"My dear girl, even a duke can feel anxious." When he paused at the window, he once more looked out on the snow-frosted world. "That was kept largely at bay by my wife's steadying presence."

"How have you managed for the past two years, then?" As much as wanted to know how his wife had died, she kept the questions to herself. Perhaps he would tell her as time went on, for if he was correct and they were stranded here, it would give them plenty of time to talk.

"I haven't." Brook rested a curled hand on the window glass and propped the other on his hip. "I rarely leave my house, and if I had a cat, I would be the perfect image of an old, doddering fool afraid of going beyond his front doorstep."

She blew out a breath. "You are not afraid; you are merely a bit lost at the moment.

And you are hardly old." Though he might be twelve years her senior, there was nothing ancient about his form. In fact, he was much too vital for her peace of mind. How would she be expected to share a room with him when he left her all too confused and dare she say excited?

"Ha! While I don't fully believe you, I appreciate the thought all the same. There are too many well-meaning people in my circle who are trying to see me matched again."

"You don't want that? After all, you will still require an heir."

"I know." A noise that was suspiciously like a sob echoed slightly in the room. The duke bowed his head and for several minutes, quiet weeping filled the air. Hope sat frozen to her chair, unsure of how to help. Finally, he heaved a long-suffering sigh. He wiped at his face with a hand, but he didn't turn. "I am not certain I can survive that risk a second time."

Before she could respond, a brief knock sounded on the door, then the panel swung open, and one of the inn's employees poked his head inside. "Mr. Gerard? If you are finished with dinner, we really do need the room, as I should clean up and set it for the next seating."

"Right." Brook turned slowly about with his pocket watch in hand. "That hour passed rather quickly." With a sigh, he looked at the footman. "Very well. We are finished here. Thank you."

After a nod, the other man disappeared, presumably to give them privacy.

Hope frowned. "What now?"

"It is seven o'clock." He returned the watch to his waistcoat pocket. "Unless you fancy sitting in the common room again, we can retire to our bedchamber for the night."

Oh, dear heavens. Tremors of unease twisted with tingles of anticipation down her spine. For what, she couldn't say, for they were certainly *not* a couple. "I suppose that is our only option. It *has* been a rather traumatic day, and I'm a bit fatigued." How would she be expected to sleep with such a man lying beside her? To say nothing of the fact she would need to undress at least to her shift, and then he would see the burn scars on her skin, realize just how horrid and ugly she truly was, know why she remained unwanted and unloved.

And if he doesn't? her mind argued as it planted a kernel of hope deep in her chest.

Then this temporary delay would be considered an adventure that would make Christmastide more tolerable before she resigned herself to the dull life awaiting her in Yorkshire.

Chapter Four

The second Brook closed the door to their shared room behind him, the feeling of awkwardness sprang between him and Hope.

This was the first time he'd had a woman with him alone since his wife died, and the knowledge didn't sit well. It didn't matter this wasn't for a tryst or any other sort of sexual assignation, the fact that Hope wasn't Deborah left him confused with knots of unease pulling in his stomach. He dumped his greatcoat and other outer things on the end of the bed. What would his wife have thought about this situation? Undoubtedly, she would have been proud he'd wished to help a young woman, but ultimately, she wouldn't have been pleased he put his reputation at risk in order to do exactly that.

"It's not luxurious, but it is shelter from the storm. We are certainly fortunate," he said as he glanced about the small space.

There was a bed that looked suspiciously lumpy beneath the counterpane spread across it. Done in muted shades of green, it was obvious

45

the bedclothes hadn't been new in quite some time. The frame wasn't that of his four-poster at home, which meant there were no curtains to pull closed about the bed and keep out the chill that was beginning to creep into the room. One solitary window occupied the far wall with drapes in the same colors as the bed at either side. A straight-backed wooden chair rested by the window with a small square table near it where a half-burned candle in a brass holder waited. By the door, a low, scratched bureau invited a guest to unpack their possessions. Another half-used candle waited atop it in a matching brass holder.

Hope cleared her throat as she rubbed her hands up and down her arms. Was she cold or simply nervous from the situation? "There is no fireplace." She put her bonnet and gloves on the chair.

He hadn't noticed that absence until she'd mentioned it. "Well, it will certainly prove an interesting night, then." The wind howled against the window, bringing with it the hiss of snow as it hit the glass. Perhaps she was merely chilly. "I suspect it will grow colder still by the time the dawn breaks." Finally, his gaze fell upon two trunks waiting off to one side of the room, partially hidden by a privacy screen and wedged near a washstand. "At least our luggage has been delivered."

"That does provide a bit of comfort, and I do have a few books tucked away in mine to pass the time." As a shiver gripped her, his companion shook from it. She had yet to remove the pelisse, but obviously she couldn't sleep in it. Such a garment would be awkward and constrictive. "There is nothing that can be done, so let us pray there are enough blankets."

"And that they do not contain fleas." Or anything else catching or disease ridden. That was the risk of staying at a posting inn, but as she said, nothing could be done. There was no other place to stay unless there might be a barn nearby, and that didn't seem as warm as a room at an inn.

"Oh, dear heavens." She raised her gaze to his. Worry clouded those brown depths, and in the shadows, she appeared much younger than her years. "I hadn't thought about that. Do you think there are other vermin in the mattress itself?"

"I truly hope not." Refusing to give into a shudder, Brook kept himself from glancing at the bed. Instead, he moved to the bureau and busied himself with lighting the candle. As soon as the flame caught on the wick, it guttered and danced due to the draft in the room. "We shall see how long this holds, but at least it dispels a bit of the darkness." Shadows leapt and danced over the walls.

"It does, though in many ways the darkness is as comforting as an old friend." Hope's eyes were round as she glanced between him and the bed. Would that he could read the thoughts racing through her head. "I suppose there is nothing else for us to do except retire."

Poor thing. Her distress was almost palpable. Was she still an innocent? He knew very little about her life before they had met outside of the snatches of what she'd told him over dinner. "Shall I take the floor?" Knowing the neighboring room was possibly occupied even at this early hour, he lowered his voice. "If you are leery of me at all, I will do this, for it wasn't your fault we are in the same room."

The delicate tendons in her throat worked with a hard swallow, but the tiny sliver of relief in her eyes didn't go unnoticed. "You shouldn't, for you are a duke and I am barely clinging to the lower level of the *ton*." She waved a hand in dismissal. "I rather doubt dukes sleep on the floor."

A certain level of humor had attached itself to the situation, but he bit the inside of his cheek to keep from laughing. "Of course they have. Dukes are people, the same as everyone else." On many levels, he didn't know what to make of her. She was attractive in a helpless, damsel-in-distress sort of way, but there was no doubt she possessed a backbone as well as a tart mouth that she would employ if the right occasion arose. Yet she was wary. Of him or the situation he didn't know. "I will survive the night."

"But it's cold enough already and will be even more so on the floor." Again, her gaze jumped between the bed and him. "*I* shall take the floor."

Damn, but it was early yet, and he hadn't adjusted to country hours. How was he expected to sleep just now? Of course, when he was in London, he did nothing except sit in his cozy leather winged-back chair and doze as soon as the sun had set…

"Nonsense, Hope. You are much slighter than I and will likely freeze." He eyed the sparse furnishings, the two pillows, the counterpane. "And I rather doubt there are blankets to spare, but I could ask the innkeeper for another set." The fact that he'd introduced himself as a commoner instead of a duke wouldn't grant him the privilege and he would no doubt return emptyhanded.

"Oh, please don't trouble yourself. No doubt others will find the night just as cold, and since the inn is full, I rather doubt there are enough supplies to go around." Her shoulders lifted in a shrug. "Once the morning comes, we can make use of the fire in the common room."

"I appreciate your practicality." Again, he thought upon the puzzle that was Hope. She was the same age Deborah had been when she'd perished during childbirth. His tiny newborn daughter had died that day as well, and still he couldn't believe he'd broken down enough in that private dining room to cry for a few minutes in front of this woman.

Obviously, grief didn't discriminate when it gripped a person.

With a shuddering sigh, Hope nodded, as if she'd had a discussion with herself in her mind. "We will share the bed." For an instant, when her gaze met his, a trace of mischief twinkled there before worry buried it. "I will behave if you will."

"Ha!" Since his wife had died, he hadn't given such things as sexual gratification a thought. "I am not seeking a romance. In fact, I don't know if I believe in that state any longer." It was perhaps more than he'd wished to share, but the words couldn't be recalled.

A frown pulled her kissable lips downward. "I understand that sentiment all too well."

What was this, then? Curiosity to know more about her history grew strong, and why the hell could he not stop staring at her mouth? "You'd hinted at a failed Season. Was there perhaps an engagement that didn't take?"

Emotions flitted over her expressionless face, but she nodded. "Unfortunately, yes."

"Do you wish to talk about it?" At least it would fill the time and stave off the inevitable fact that they would need to share a bed.

"Not at the moment." Again, she rubbed her hands up and down her arms. With a sigh that smacked of resignation, she moved to the window and drew the drapes closed. The gloom in the room intensified. "We should probably undress and retire."

"Have you grown bored with my company already?" Though he'd meant to infuse the inquiry with humor, the attempt at a joke fell flat.

"Not by half." A grin flirted with her lips. "While I suspect you are an interesting man in your own right, unless you wish to teach me how to play cards or how to wager, there is nothing else to do." She manipulated the buttons at the front of her pelisse. "I rather suspect we have little enough in common to talk about."

A trace of cold disappointment went through his chest. "Well, that is somewhat of a letdown. I have always prided myself on my ability to draw people from whatever walk of life into conversation." But perhaps she had a point. There were merely strangers, after all.

"Oh, bother." A huff of frustration left her throat as she shrugged out of the pelisse. "Please don't mind me. I am rather prickly just now due to this situation and the storm. The sound of the wind is quite forlorn and only serves to remind me of my plight." When she glanced across the bed at him with the garment hanging over her arm, worry etched itself through her expression. "Never did I think I would need to fret over my future as I do right now. And I certainly hadn't anticipated the possibility of being anyone's companion."

"Are you not the nurturing type, then?" The dulcet tones of her voice were a pleasant, soothing melody, and he'd forgotten how lovely it was to listen to a woman speak.

"It isn't that." As she draped the pelisse over the back of the chair, he was treated to her form in profile. Slender but with gentle curves that would tempt any man to sin, he couldn't understand why she hadn't married. Was the engagement failure her fault or that of the man's? When she straightened and faced him, there wasn't nothing at all alluring about the traveling dress of maroon wool she wore. It covered her from wrist to neck. So why had he been ready to wax poetic over her form? "I do enjoy taking care of people and did so often enough with my family. However…"

"Yes?" One of his eyebrows arched when her words trailed off.

"Eventually, I would like to know what it feels like to have someone look after me for once." A blush rose into her pale cheeks that worked to further give mystery to her pixie's face. "My parents did that, of course, yet the kindness has been all too absent since they left this world."

"I am sorry to hear that." Her life and his had been very different, except they had common grief to bind them. While he struggled out of his tight-fitting jacket, he thought upon the scenario from her perspective. No doubt she was terrified and a bit at sixes and sevens. There truly weren't many choices for a young woman without means or decent family. "You have my promise I will look after you for as long as our paths converge." At least he could give her that.

"Thank you." With a nod and the shy duck of her head, she moved toward the faded silk privacy screen. "If you will excuse me?"

"Of course." The rustle of fabric indicated she'd decided to undress behind the screen, and he couldn't fault her for that. Once Hope hung the dress over the frame, two full thuds echoed in the space. Perhaps she'd removed her half boots.

Brook concentrated on his own toilette. A groan of relief escaped him when he took off his own boots. It had been a bit on an endeavor without the aid of his valet, but he accomplished it and thrilled slightly at the personal victory. His waistcoat soon followed and joined his jacket at the foot of the bed. While he worked at his cuffs, collar, and cravat, the sound of splashing water sounded from the wash basin. When he glanced in that direction, an unexpected rush of desire went down his spine to lodge in his stones, for she was garbed only in her shift. Though her backside was toward him as she washed her hands and face, in the guttering candlelight it was possible to discern the outline of her thighs beneath the thin garment.

Bloody hell.

Once she'd finished, Hope came out from around the screen. Due to the chilly temperature in the room, the outline of her erect nipples was clearly evident through the shift. Spying those pink tips temporarily stole his ability to speak, but he couldn't help but sweep his gaze over the rest of her figure.

Yes, now that she was free of the stifling dress, the curves he'd originally spied were evident—soft swell of the hips set off by a narrow waist. If she were to bedeck herself in the latest styles of ballgowns, she would easily be a Diamond of the First Water. Unfortunately, his attention was pulled to the shadow of dark hair at the apex of her thighs, just barely a hint in the candlelight.

Awareness of her shivered through his shaft. *Well, damn.*

Seeing her thusly was all too suggestive and served as a stark reminder they were both walking the thin line into scandal, so he yanked his gaze up her body as she stared back at him with confusion in her eyes. He took in the tops of her modest, creamy breasts, noted how delicate her bare arms were, but on the inside of her right arm, the pale skin was mottled and marred by what looked to be burn marks. When she caught him staring at the area, she immediately turned in an effort to hide the arm from his view.

"I apologize for being rude," he murmured. What else was there to say?

"Think nothing of it, Your Grace."

The return to formality rankled more than it should have, but it had been crude to ogle her. Still, what the devil had happened to mar that beautiful skin? Though curious, he declined to ask, for it obviously made her embarrassed. Then he busied himself with removing his fine lawn shirt as he racked his brain for something erudite to say. In short order, the garment was tossed to the growing pile at the foot of the bed. "I suppose I should relieve myself before tucking into bed. There is nothing worse than wriggling into a comfortable position and realizing an urgent need to urinate."

It was hardly a conversation to have in mixed company, and he sounded like a raving lunatic by doing so, but she snickered, and when his arm brushed hers as they maneuvered around each other and the bed so he could gain the privacy screen, tingling heat went up his limb to his elbow.

The faint scent of violets wafted to his nose. The flower and the elusive perfume suited her delicate frame. "Pardon me." She gained the side of the bed, quickly scooted beneath the bedclothes, and then looked at him with questions in those damned doe eyes that could make a man do many wicked, scandalous things.

"It *is* rather cramped quarters," he whispered as he retreated behind the privacy screen with a sigh of relief. After he'd taken care of the immediate needs of his body, Brook stood at the washstand and splashed his face with the icy water from the basin. The jarring temperature did nothing to cool the immediate and unexpected desire that had caught him by surprise merely from seeing her in that shift.

Get hold of yourself, Denton. You are not looking for love, romance, or even a quick roll in the sheets.

While this was true, no amount of self-chastisement would settle the interest in his shaft. Eventually, he dried his hands and returned to the room at large. Hope held the bedclothes up to her chin as she watched him, and when it became obvious she studied his form as openly as he'd done to her, heat rose up the back of his neck. Did he pass muster? For that matter, why did he care what she thought of his looks? Nothing would happen between them.

"Do you mind if I extinguish the candle?"

"Please do. The darkness is preferrable just now." She slowly sent her gaze down his body, and when it glanced over the front of his breeches, he held his breath. Could she see his semi-hard member that pressed against the fabric?

"I hope it isn't my presence you object to," he said, went to the bureau and then swiftly blew out the candle.

"Of course not, but you might object to *me* if you only knew…" Once more, her words trailed off, and damn if it wasn't annoying.

"Such gammon."

The room was plunged into shadows. Not even the drapes at the window muted the sound of the howling wind or the hiss of snow against the glass. How long would the storm rage, and how many days would they spend stranded together at this inn? He sat heavily on his side of the bed, tried to calm his response to her presence and perusal.

Already, there was a decided chill in the air. The cold trailed over his bare chest, and he welcomed the opportunity to cool the fire licking through his blood. What the devil was wrong with him? The first time he was in close proximity to a woman and his body reacted as if he were naught but a primal animal?

You are better than this, Denton.

With nothing for it, Brook slipped beneath the bedclothes, and as he settled onto his back, felt more than a few lumps in the bed, he stifled a sigh. Beside him, Hope shifted, and the heat of her seemed to reach out and touch him. Though the sheets and blankets were soft enough and smelled decently clean, they were a bit scratchy against his skin and they probably wouldn't provide enough warmth, but he would worry about that later. The more immediate concern was the willful cockstand he sported, merely because there was a woman beside him.

Damned annoying, is what it was. Though, truth to tell, the experience was both odd and thrilling. He missed having a woman in bed, for he'd never taken a mistress since he'd wed, and he certainly hadn't encouraged anyone to service him following the death of his wife. If the urge had become too difficult to ignore, he'd usually taken himself in hand; there was no shame in it. Spending was a natural bodily function, yet continued arousal would make for a long night.

God help him if the night grew into a few due to the storm.

"Goodnight, Hope. May the night keep you well." Though the idea of sharing a bed with a woman who was a relative stranger rankled, there was a certain comfort in speaking to her while hidden in the shadows.

Perhaps it was one of those niceties he missed the most of not being married.

The bedclothes rustled again. She briefly touched his arm, and that tiny reminder of their current deception streaked through his body to further tighten his length. "Sleep well, Brook. And thank you. Sharing a bed with you is vastly preferable to whatever else awaited me."

He allowed a smile in the darkness. "You are quite welcome." Then he stared up at the ceiling to watch the shifting shadows while waiting for his erection to settle.

Would that the night wouldn't prove long.

Chapter Five

❖━━━❖❖❖━━━❖

December 22, 1810
Somewhat after midnight

The howling of the wind was such a lonely, mournful sound that it haunted Hope's dreams and infiltrated her mind, lending mystery and a thread of danger to her thoughts that she came awake with a slight moan.

For a few moments, she didn't remember where she was. The bed felt strange and lumpy in spots, and the pillow didn't quite cradle her head and neck like it should. Obviously, she wasn't at home in London, and when a chilly draft of air wafted across her cheek, she gave into a full-body shiver.

Then she remembered.

Of course she was no longer in London. She hadn't been for a few days. Her uncle had encouraged her to take a position as companion, and she was traveling there, scheduled to arrive in Yorkshire just ahead of Christmas.

No longer would she spend the days wrapped in familial comfort and love with her family, for her parents were dead which had left her an unwanted relation.

Unwanted by the only family she had left to her.

Unloved by her fiancé, who'd taken one look at her burn scars and had begged off in the most cowardly way possible. The finality of those words in the letter left a bitterness and grief in her blood. Over and over, they echoed in her mind.

"…I am not certain I can bring myself to touch those scars…"

"…I am afraid I must move on…"

"…there is another to whom my affection lies more…"

Wasn't love supposed to render scars and such markings invisible to a betrothed eye? The one time she had let a man see her in a state of undress, as soon as he'd looked upon the patches of twisted, mottled skin, had accidentally brushed his fingers over the raised flesh on the inside of her right arm, he'd recoiled with revulsion.

Perhaps it hadn't been love between them after all. The engagement might have collapsed on its own if she hadn't been scarred… or it could have strengthened into love, but it didn't matter now. She would never know what could have been, for with the advent of that letter, rumor held that he'd immediately began courting another woman.

Which had begun her long, tedious descent into the realm of being undesired. The only future left for her was that of an elderly lady's companion. How long she would survive the position was anyone's guess, but she rather doubted the holiday season would hold much joy or comfort, and the loneliness she'd carried ever since her parents had perished would only grow.

In her half-awake state, Hope thrashed her head upon the pillow. Her hands clenched at the bedclothes as if those meager blankets could act as a shield to keep her from both harm and the dull monotony that life would undoubtedly become.

Except, the storm had waylaid travel. Reaching Yorkshire would be postponed by a few days, especially if the storm held.

Another gust of wind slammed against the side of the inn. The windowpane rattled and the soft sting of snow against the glass infiltrated her thoughts. A shiver lanced down her spine.

Not quite fully awake, she moaned again as thoughts zipped quickly through her mind. No, she wasn't at home, but instead, the coach broke a wheel. She'd walked to The Brown Hare Inn. There were no rooms. A duke had taken pity on her. They were pretending to be a married couple, forced to share a bed because she didn't want him on the cold floor.

He'd seen the burn scars on her arm but had said nothing. What did he think? Dear God, what would he say if he ever saw the scars on her belly, abdomen, and her right hip? They were even more hideous than the one on her arm. Hot saliva filled her mouth, for he undoubtedly thought her repulsive, just like her fiancé had. *How can I face him in the morning?* This man who still mourned his dead wife, who hadn't needed to protect her from the general public at the inn, whose torso had been the most beautiful thing she'd seen in ever so a long time.

The duke would face serious consequences if anyone in the *ton* ever found out about his stint in this room with her. It was too much a chance for him to take when he knew nothing about her. She might not have much of a future, but he did.

A whimper escaped her. Hope turned onto her side with her back firmly to the duke as he slept on. No doubt he couldn't wait to be rid of her, to be done with his task of escorting her to Yorkshire and giving her over into his aunt's care. Dear God, but she missed her parents! Missed knowing that no matter where she was in England, she would have a home to return to, someone to talk with, to receive comfort from. But there was nothing like that for her. It was her lot in life to pass the remainder of her existence alone—unwanted and unloved—because she was hideous and couldn't attract a husband.

How had events become so far off course?

A few tears slipped to her cheeks, and she left them to slide down. When she tried to stifle the next whimper, it was a dismal attempt at best. Heat of mortification crept into her cheeks. What if her crying woke the duke and he heard? Oh, he would surely think her a young and immature ninny, when she should be grateful she had a position to go to at all.

"Come here, love. It cannot be as bad as that." Then Brook's arms were around her. He pulled her into the middle of the bed and held her against the hard wall of his body.

Hope's mind spun from the endearment, but she was more than certain he hadn't meant her when he'd uttered it. For the moment, her tears were forgotten. "Oh, but it is," she said into the darkness. "Despite my name, I am feeling rather hopeless." He was so warm and all too comforting as she lay stiffly in his embrace, her backside securely nestled to his front.

It was both exciting and somewhat disconcerting.

"There is *always* hope." His chuckle rang in her ear and reverberated in her chest.

"I am not so sure." Knowing this highly scandalous yet infinitely wonderful at the same time, she remained frozen with indecision.

Logic told her she should push out of his embrace, for he wasn't quite awake, but the part of her brain that held tight to fantasy and fairy stories encouraged her to linger, for it was doubtful she would ever experience the joy of a man's arms around her again. "This is not proper, Your Grace."

Again, he chuckled, and the sound was much like melted drinking chocolate she'd had once for breakfast while with her uncle during that glorious Season. It was luxurious and she wished she could lose herself in it. "This hasn't been proper since I put forth the idea that we are a married couple."

"Then you should release me," she said in a soft voice the darkness of the room swallowed up as soon as the words were uttered.

"At least let me give you some comfort, for I, too, know how difficult this time of the year is when life has come unsorted." The timbre of his tone sent a host of tingles down her spine. His breath warmed the shell of her ear. "When one doesn't have family about, the loneliness creeps in to remind us we are different, that we no longer have love." If she hadn't been paying attention, she wouldn't have noticed the tiny catch in his voice.

But it was there, and it made him so much more relatable. He might be a duke and she a nobody in the *ton*, yet they shared a bond of grief and a life that stretched into emptiness. His coffers were full and hers nonexistent, but in this they were on the same level ground.

"That doesn't mean it will always be like this, Your Grace." She sucked in a breath of surprise when he splayed a hand against her stomach, preventing her from moving away from him while the other rested casually at her left hip.

"I wish I could believe that." Slowly, almost abstractedly, he strummed his fingers along her hip. "My name is Brook. You made use of it before."

"So I did." Her eyelids drooped, for the warmth of him, the repetitive movements of his fingers, the graveled roughness of the sleep in his voice all worked to relax her, and with a sigh she snuggled deeper into the bedding. "Thank you, Brook. I don't feel so alone just now."

"Good." For long moments, the only sound in the room was the ever-present wind blowing outside and the duke's even exhalations. His breath skated over her cheek, then he shifted slightly, and that breath warmed her nape. "No one should feel alone at Christmastide." He stroked his fingers over her hip, leaving gooseflesh in his wake. At the same time, the hand on her belly glanced up and down between her naval and her breasts.

Merciful heavens! Was he even aware of what he did? Her nipples tightened. Tiny fires licked through her blood from the unexpected caresses. Perhaps it didn't matter, for his touch—intentional or not—chased away the chill.

"Do you think we'll be stranded here until Christmas?" She hated to even ask and possibly disturb the tranquil excitement of the moment, but then another gust of wind hit the window, and she shivered. Oh, how she detested the harsh coldness of winter! It was as if nature was peering into her soul and seeing the harsh truth of her existence.

"Perhaps, but there is no use worrying over it. We cannot control the weather." The duke shifted his position and better spooned her body with his. When the insistent hardness of his member pressed against her bottom, tingles of awareness tripped down her spine. Would he have felt such a reaction to any woman in his bed, or was that merely because of *her* proximity?

"No, I suppose not." No longer did she wish to put space between them on the bed, for being in his arms, having his form pressed so intimately to hers was simply too lovely to destroy.

"Enjoy this time. Rarely are we given such a boon as not having a schedule to keep." Then he nuzzled the crook of her shoulder. The hand on her hip gathered the fabric of her shift and slowly drew the hem up her leg.

Hope froze. Her breath stalled in her throat as foreign sensations zipped from the roots of her hair to the tips of her toes. Though she'd shared one embrace with her fiancé, had granted him liberties and gave the same before he'd begged off the engagement, that long ago episode hadn't made her feel both hot and cold at the same time as the duke's sleep-drugged exploration did. Still, scandal lay this way, and if word got out it might destroy her chances of landing the companion position.

What would she do then?

For that matter, what should she do *now*? As his nuzzling continued and his fingers at her hip encountered bare skin, a sigh of pure enjoyment escaped her. There was no harm in letting him think whatever he did, for she would make certain the embrace didn't grow into full-blown gossip. When she wriggled and her bottom bumped his erection, the groan that shivered from him heightened her awareness of him.

"Brook?"

"Shh." He continued to nuzzle the crook of her shoulder while caressing her thigh. "The night is less frightening when you are not alone." Did that mean the darkness left him worried as well? There was no way to tell. The only thing she knew for certain was that each touch he gave her left her trembling with a need she didn't fully understand.

The fact she didn't dissuade him confused her, but then she stopped thinking altogether, for his fingers drifted to the curls shrouding her sex. Her breathing increased. Oh, good heavens, *what* did he intend? And would she let him if he went further? She didn't know. Instead, Hope enjoyed having a man's hands on her, working to relax her and keep her worries at bay.

When he peppered the underside of her jaw with feather-weighted kisses, a slight moan escaped her, and she lifted her chin to allow him greater access. The rasp of his evening stubble sent a rush of need through her system. What would that feel like against the more sensitive parts of her body? Would there ever be an opportunity to know?

His fingers danced over her skin between her mons and her hip, never quite venturing between her thighs, but just thinking about what that might be like left her quivering with anticipation. Daring much, Hope slightly turned into him, and he rewarded the effort by gliding his lips along the side of her neck. Gentle nips and nibbles followed that made her catch her breath. Tingles fell down her spine, for the attention, the little bursts of pleasure he imparted were so startling that it was so obvious at how neglected she had been over the years.

"Mmm." She managed to rest a palm against his naked chest. What she wouldn't give to have the right to explore his body. What would his skin feel like, taste like to her lips, her tongue? "This is lovely." It was also folly to allow it to continue, but she couldn't bear to bid him nay. All her life she'd yearned to discover what being wanted—claimed—by a man felt like.

"The night was made for kissing." One of his hands drift upward to cup her breast. Hope gasped as she adjusted to the feel of his palm against her hardened nipple. The heat of his fingers seemed to sear through the fabric of her shift. Pleasure rippled out from the hardened bud he rubbed his fingertips over. Her altered position made it all too easy for him to slip the fingers of his free hand between her slightly parted thighs. Heated tingles moved through her lower belly. "Ah, love, it has been too long. I have missed you."

A chill moved down Hope's spine. *Oh, dear Lord.* In his half-sleeping state, did he assume he was with his dead wife? Was he indeed drifting in and out of a dream even as he was touching, caressing, kissing *her*? No matter how wonderful it felt to be in his arms or letting him have intimate access to her, all the fun and excitement of the moment faded if he thought her someone else. *This isn't right.*

"Brook?" She shoved at his shoulder, but he didn't wake. "Your Grace? You must leave off." With a hand pressed firmly to his chest, she pushed at his body. "This isn't right. I am *not* your wife." Goodness but she hated the catch in her voice. Of course she couldn't inspire a man

Sandra Sookoo

like him to passion for her own self. If he hadn't been lost to memories and dreams, would he have done the same?

Unfortunately, Hope already suspected the answer.

He came fully awake with a gasp and a soft curse. "Hope?" The duke immediately tore himself away from her and sat up in the bed. The covers slid down his torso, and she couldn't help but stare at his chest even though it was shrouded by shadows. "Dear God, please tell me I didn't violate you." Horror rang in the inquiry, and it sent a ball of tears into her throat.

"You did not." Was she so hideous, then, that the thought of doing exactly that turn his stomach? To stave off tears, she cleared her throat. "I suspect you merely wished to offer me comfort when I awoke disoriented and frightened from the storm and in a strange place." The lie was needed to set him at ease. Not for worlds would she admit to what he'd really done or how much she had enjoyed it.

"Ah. I apologize all the same." He slid from the bed quickly as if she might bite him. "I sometimes dream of my wife, and sometimes those dreams are so real, so vivid I can see her, touch her, and then I remember…"

"There is no need for an explanation, Your Grace." His explanation was heart wrenching, but she understood. Often, she'd taken refuge into dreams when life had been far

71

kinder and simpler, and there was no struggle with reality.

"All the same, I shall pass the remainder of the night on the floor. Be assured, nothing like this will happen again."

"But I... You didn't..." There was no point in continuing to talk, for he plucked up his pillow and dropped it onto the floor. "Please, Brook, return to the bed. You'll freeze down there." The chill in the air was more pronounced now than it had been when they'd settled into sleep. Thankful for the clinging darkness that hopefully hid her aroused nipples, she moved closer to his side of the bed. "Truly, I took no offense."

"All the same, it is better to remove temptation—accidental or otherwise." The man snatched his greatcoat from the foot of the bed and quickly donned it. "Good night, Miss Atwater. I trust the remainder of your sleep will prove uninterrupted." Then he laid down upon the floor, and it was several minutes before his tossing and turning stilled.

With a stifled cry, Hope burrowed back into the bedclothes on her side of the bed. The warmth of being held in his arms had faded all too quickly, and she shivered. It was only fitting she ended the day very much as she'd started it—alone with her thoughts.

Just once why can I not know what it's like to be fully needed and wanted — for myself?

Sandra Sookoo

Chapter Six

December 22, 1810
An hour after sunrise

Brook came awake on the floor with stiff muscles and an aching back, but his first thought was of Hope and what he'd done to her last night.

Good God, he'd touched her without her consent, put his hands and lips on her, all because he'd heard her crying in the night. What had started out as a need to comfort her had slipped into something that should never have happened, for he'd been halfway lost to sleep, and he owed her an apology.

Several, if he were honest. Perhaps it would have been better if he'd never put forth the bit of fiction they were a married couple.

Yet at some point during the night, he'd dreamed of his wife, much as he always did, and once more she'd beckoned to him, imploring him with her eyes to join her. Those were the nights that sent him into grief more than the others, when he missed her so much, couldn't imagine going through the remainder of his life without her. Some would call those dreams nightmares, and perhaps sometimes they were, for he usually woke to the horror that she was truly gone.

Except this morning. His thoughts hadn't lingered on Deborah. Instead, he'd had visions of Hope in his mind, knew he immediately needed to talk with her instead of linger in dreams of things that once were.

Trying to ignore the chill in the air, he rose from the makeshift pallet on the floor and wrapped his greatcoat about his body. As of yet, Hope was still abed with the covers tucked up around her chin while she lay curled on her side. She seemed so small and fragile—lost perhaps— that it only added to the hot guilt swirling inside his chest.

He moved to the window, and upon opening the drapes peered outside toward the wooded area. Several inches of snow had fallen overnight, which was unprecedented, for England didn't usually see that much precipitation, especially this early in the season. And damn if the wind wasn't still blowing. It kicked up some of the whiteness, swirled it about before depositing it deeper into the tree line. What the roads looked like, he couldn't say, but likely were a mess.

When the bedclothes rustled and she uttered garbled words, Brook turned to face her. "What time is it?"

He glanced to the foot of the bed where he'd left his waistcoat, which still contained his pocket watch. "I cannot say for certain but surely an hour or so past dawn." Again, he peered out the window. "No sun to speak of today. More clouds and snow while the wind continues to whip over the land."

"Oh." She didn't sound pleased regarding the prospect. Then her round-eyed gaze found his. "How did you pass the night?"

"Terribly, I'm afraid." At least it was honest. "Cold. And it wasn't comfortable."

"You shouldn't have removed from the bed."

"It was necessary after the way I behaved." With a tight chest, he moved closer and finally perched on the very edge of the bed, far enough away that he wouldn't be tempted to touched her. "I violated your trust."

"You did not." Her slight shrug sent the bedclothes slipping down her body. They paused at the slope of her breasts, and he held his breath. Would they fall further? "I could have bid you nay at any point, and regardless, no harm was done."

Then why couldn't he evict those memories from his mind? Even now, the remembered heat of her body against his brought both comfort and awareness. As best he could, Brook tamped the thoughts. "Are you feeling better than you were last night? I woke to the sound of your whimpering, assumed you were in distress." Hadn't it been logical to take her into his arms and offer support the best way he knew how?

"Perhaps a bit." Her gaze dropped to the counterpane. The fact she wouldn't look at him sent more censure hurtling through his chest. "At least it is morning. That which haunts us at night is never as acute in the daytime hours."

God, I'm a bounder. He frowned. What demons did she struggle with? "Now that we are both awake, I'd like to offer my apologies to you. Again. I didn't mean to—"

"Stop, Your Grace." Hope raised her head. Nothing except honesty shone in those brown eyes. "Truly, there is nothing to apologize for." She cocked her head to one side. "The night was chilly and a tad bit spooky. I was glad I wasn't alone. However, if you are worried I'll cry foul and demand you marry me, set those fears to rest. Those aren't my intentions, and neither am I interested in that."

"I appreciate your candor." He nodded, and as a thread of relief twisted down his spine, he frowned. "Is it me, then, you take exception to or the wedded state itself?" Perhaps this was an opportunity to learn more about her.

A blush stained her cheeks, and in the morning gloom with the caramel strands glimmering in her brown hair, she was wholesomely beautiful, and he wished he knew how to paint portraits. "Trust me when I say my reticence isn't with you."

Unexpected pleasure curled through his chest. It was damned cold in the room except for when he thought about or looked at her. That in and of itself was troublesome. "You don't wish to marry, then?"

"I suppose if someone were to ask, I would seriously consider the union, for I don't wish to spend my life alone, even if that possibility has been thrust upon me." A trace of sadness went through her eyes. "However, I have been shown that certain aspects of... me are unpalatable, which makes me invisible to marriage-minded men."

How odd. "You speak of the scarring on your arm." It wasn't a question, and when his gaze moved to that limb, she hid it beneath the bedclothes.

"It is not just my arm." Again, she looked away. "That scarring covers a portion of my side, belly, abdomen, and leg on the right side of my body." The delicate tendons in her throat worked with a hard swallow. "My, uh, fiancé couldn't apparently tolerate them, couldn't see past them to who I was," she admitted in a whispered voice.

"Then that man wasn't honorable enough to be with you." Surprise from the conviction in his voice lifted one of his eyebrows. Where had that outburst stemmed from? "Men who fail to see the worth of a woman in her full potential have lost my respect."

A tiny smile curved her lips, and he well remembered the sounds of surprise and pleasure she'd made in the night. If he were to kiss her, what would those lips feel like? Such thinking was dangerous, and he really should quell any further urges. "Thank you. I appreciate the defense."

"Every woman is beautiful in her own way, Hope. Don't forget that." He met her gaze, and once more, those brown pools invited him closer. "We are not what happened to us."

When a trace of tears appeared in her eyes, his chest tightened, for he felt so ineffectual. "That is a good reminder, Your Grace."

Possessed of possible madness, Brook relocated on her side of bed, close enough to take the hand she hadn't hidden beneath the bedclothes. "My name is Brook."

"I know, but I forget. Being in a duke's company, those manners are ingrained."

The need to hear her utter the word grew strong. "Say it."

Confusion lined her expression. "Your name?"

"Yes." Gently, he tightened his hold on her hand. The memory of how her breast had felt against his palm, the insistent stiffness of her nipple between his fingers had his imagination dancing and fire licking through his veins. What the devil was wrong with him?

"Brook." She leaned toward him with her lips ever so slightly parted and the bedclothes sliding further down her chest. "I shall try to remember for next time."

"Good." For the space of a few heartbeats, they remained like that until reality set in. He immediately released her hand and scrambled to his feet. "We should probably dress."

"Of course." She glanced toward the privacy screen where her traveling outfit from the day before remaining hanging over the frame. "Do you want to attend to the necessary first?"

"Please, go ahead. I don't mind waiting." Out of deference to her privacy, he should have looked away when she exited the bed, but he didn't, and the quick chance to see her in that shift when she wasn't shrouded in darkness was every bit as wonderful as he thought it would be. Her peach-hued skin showed through the thin fabric and there was a glimpse of a nipple before she vanished behind the privacy screen. "Well, damn," he said beneath his breath and then moved to the end of the bed.

"Is everything well, Your... er, Brook?"

The way she said his name, as if the word almost purred from her throat, sent a shiver of awareness down his spine. "Yes, of course. I am trying to acclimate to the chill while dressing." So saying, he removed his greatcoat and then made quick work of donning his shirt. He tried not to think about anything while the rustle of fabric hinted at the fact that she was dressing.

Why, all of a sudden, after just over two years since losing his wife was he bedeviled by a woman he'd only just met?

Barely had he struggled into his waistcoat and manipulated the laces behind him as best he could than Hope moved out from behind the screen to stand at the washstand.

A snort escaped her. "The water in the basin is frozen."

"I warned you it was cold." He joined her in the small space and peered into the basin. Sure enough, the shallow depth of the water was completely solid. Hope had tidied her hair, and once more it was properly contained into an unassuming knot at the back of her head. "It was my original intention to have a light breakfast brought up to the room, but perhaps we should go down to the common room where the fire is burning."

Interest lit her eyes. "Agreed, but I must tell you. I might require more food than what a light breakfast will provide." As if to support her claim, her stomach growled.

They both laughed, and the sound dispelled the growing tension between them.

"I think that can be arranged, for I am rather hungry as well." Again, he marveled over how different she was from Deborah. His wife had rarely tucked into a meal with gusto. Usually, she picked at her food, claiming to not have an appetite, but he secretly thought she didn't wish to gain weight, for the *ton's* eyes always scrutinized woman, especially a duchess.

"Good." She stared up at him, and it was driven home to him how petite she was. Perhaps barely standing a couple inches over five feet. "Did you, ah, wish to have assistance with your jacket?"

"That would be helpful. Yes." As if she would burn him, he darted out of the area in order to retrieve his jacket. "These garments are tailored so tightly a man can hardly don them without making a fool of himself."

"It seems the more expensive the cut, the more difficult the clothing." She tugged the jacket from his fingers. "Turnabout, please."

As he did so and she held up the garment, the muscles in his belly contracted. Deborah used to help him sometimes with his jackets. He'd rather missed the little intimacy of the act. The second he slipped his arms into the sleeves, and Hope spread her hands across his back to smooth out the fit, awareness of her shivered down his spine.

"Again, I apologize for my trespass last night." It was important that she understood it wasn't his habit to accost every woman he came across.

"Brook, please." She released a huff of frustration while facing him. "Stop. I needed the comfort; you apparently needed to have a woman close by. There was no harm in the situation." There was a longing in her eyes and a sadness he suddenly wished to investigate. "I wasn't offended, and quite frankly, I enjoyed the companionship."

"I..." Learning to interact with this slip of a young woman was leaving him tongue-tied and confused, to say nothing of feeling things he hadn't let himself experience for far too long. While she manipulated the buttons of the jacket, a tremble of need went up his spine. "I... forgot myself, thought for a few minutes my wife wasn't dead... that I might have imagined that whole horrible day when she left."

It was the closest he'd ever come to talking about that day with anyone. And perhaps he might like to continue if she was willing.

"Oh, Brook." Compassion flitted through in her expression. Understanding clouded her eyes as she once more met his gaze. "I am sorry. I cannot imagine losing a spouse." Her fingers lingered a few seconds too long on his buttons. That warmth only heightened his errant hunger.

There had been something about the mystery of the dark that had made it seem as if anything was possible, which was what had prodded him to kiss and caress his faux wife.

If given the opportunity again, would he do the same? Honestly, he didn't know.

"It was a terrible time in my life I hope to never repeat." With cold regret pooling in his belly, he stepped away and put much needed distance between them on the pretense of donning his boots.

"Loss is terrible, and grief is even more poignant at this time of year, when families gather." Hope rooted around on the floor until she found her half-boots. Gingerly, she perched on the edge of the straight-backed chair. "This year will be odd without the traditions I have grown accustomed to."

Suddenly, he wished to know much more about her and the life she'd led before all the hurts and disappointments had made an indelible impression. "I quite agree. When the people we love are taken from us unexpectedly, they leave a void behind, and though we might crave their presence again, the reality is very different."

He sat heavily on the bed and tugged the first boot onto his left foot while he battled to keep his emotions at bay. He'd thought they'd been under control, but that scab had been ripped open with the advent of this one young woman who wasn't afraid to show her own vulnerability.

"There is one bright spot the storm has brought, though." If the cheerfulness in her voice sounded forced, he didn't comment upon it.

"Oh?" Brook shoved his right foot into the remaining boot.

Hope came into his line of sight, and he silently cursed that the drab garment she wore hid the best aspects of her figure. "We are together. Not just you and I, but the rest of the travelers stranded in this inn. No doubt they are suffering from the same bouts of loneliness and ennui we are. Perhaps for different reasons, but they are away from their plans and their families all the same."

"I hadn't thought of it in that way before. Thank you for that." It wasn't the first time she'd opened his eyes to see something in a different perspective. The knowledge that he still had much to learn left him both humbled and excited. "Are you ready for breakfast? I believe I am going to order a pot of tea and tell the innkeeper to keep them coming." Truly, he was chilled to the bone.

"I am."

"Good." He allowed himself a small grin as he brought her to the door. Once out in the dimly lit corridor, he offered her his arm bent at the elbow. "Here is hoping we pass a pleasant morning, Mrs. Gerard."

"Indeed, Mr. Gerard." Another blush sank into her cheeks.

It was rather lovely seeing how quickly she went to sixes and sevens. Instead of dreading the remainder of the trip to Yorkshire playing as her escort until they reached his aunt's home, he looked forward to it. Would he linger there in an effort to see her settled? And if he did, would that draw the attention of his aunt's blistering tongue? That remained to be seen, but he rather thought it might be worth having a few more days in Hope's company. "Do you wish for a private dining room this morning?" That was, *if* he could secure one.

"No, thank you. It might be fun to observe our fellow travelers in the daylight."

By the time they were settled at a table near the fire and had ordered their repast, his maudlin spirits had fled. There was something about Hope that made him feel almost cheerful, dare he say hopeful despite the years of grief he'd previously labored under.

She turned her bright gaze to him and looked for all the world as if she knew a secret but hadn't yet shared it. "What have you planned for today? I really don't feel like doing handiwork and the wind makes it difficult to concentrate on reading."

The fact she deferred to him—*included* him—in whatever they did tightened his chest with unexpected gratitude. "We could stroll through the common room."

"That would only occupy twenty minutes. I'd rather not have the day stretch out endlessly."

"Whatever happened to wishing to bond with your fellow stranded travelers?" It was easy to tease her, and when she laughed, he wanted to hear much more of that tinkling sound.

"Just now, there are nothing except questionable personages in the room."

A quick glance had him concurring. Mostly men, some more unkempt than others, occupied a few of the tables as they talked—or rather complained—about whatever misery was popular at the moment. "But they are undoubtedly lonely, Hope. I'm sure you could entertain them if you put your mind to it."

"Do hush, Denton," she said softly while she eyed him askance. "That is cruel and unusual punishment."

A laugh escaped him before he could recall it. God, how long had it been since he'd found anything amusing? His spirits lifted further. "I could read to you. Didn't you say you had brought books with you?"

"Perhaps later." She sighed and once more looked through the common area. "What else is there to do?"

"Hmm." When she landed her gaze back on him, Brook waggled his eyebrows. "I could teach you how to play faro or whist. Promise to keep that knowledge to yourself. If my aunt were to find out that I'd corrupted you, we'll both land in the kettle for certain."

The boredom in her expression immediately cleared. "That is quite an acceptable way to pass the time."

"Good. What would you have eventually done if I hadn't suggested that?"

She shrugged. "Most likely I would have brought my notebook and pencil down from the room." Another blush filled her cheeks. "When I am bored or need to occupy my mind, I have recently begun to write fictional stories about the people I meet in my daily life. That has then given me the confidence to pen other sorts of stories that have nothing to do with real people." Embarrassment crossed her face. "I rather enjoy the challenge of it."

"You are a writer." By Jove, that was the best thing he'd heard all month. "How lovely. I have often wondered how an author puts together a good yarn."

"I haven't had anything published, so I don't know how proficient I am at the craft. It's merely scribbling yet, but I find studying human nature fascinating."

"No one is a master right out of the gate, Mrs. Gerard." Again, he waggled his eyebrows, and when she gave him a genuine smile, he returned the gesture.

This could be trouble... if he let it, and that would largely depend on how much willpower he exerted.

Damn it.

Chapter Seven

December 22, 1810
Just after eight o'clock in the evening

Hope yawned as she preceded the duke up the stairs toward their room that night.

She and Brook had spent the day together—since the innkeeper and his staff thought them husband and wife anyway—and whether it was in the common room, a private dining room, or in the room they shared to play cards or talk about desultory things, it had been a refreshing change to passing the time in a post chaise.

The man had a latent sense of humor, and yes, she had to work to bring it to the forefront, but once he discovered it, was encouraged to use it or to even laugh, he was quite a lovely companion. Yet there were other times when their conversations lagged, and he lapsed into brooding silence where she could only assume he thought about his wife. Still, she enjoyed being with him, had even managed to best him at two hands of faro.

Did she wish to learn more about him? Absolutely, even if that meant she would need to return the favor and share her own pain. Perhaps that would help him to open up and work through some of the grief he held on to.

"Hope?"

"Hmm?" She frowned as she stared at the closed door to their shared room. When had they completed the trip up the stairs?

"Are you well? You have been looking at the door for the last several seconds but haven't opened it." Concern threaded through his voice.

She startled, for his breath warmed her nape. Having him so close sent awareness prickling over her skin. "Oh." In some confusion she glanced at the panel and then over her shoulder at him. "I suppose I'm woolgathering."

"Assembling those stories in your head, no doubt." The duke reached around her, pressed the tarnished brass handle, and then pushed the door open. "After you, Mrs. Gerard."

"Thank you." It wasn't her fiction writing that had apparently put maggots into her brain. Instead, she couldn't banish Brook from her thoughts. Spending so much of her time with him, watching him as he'd talked to a few people in the common room, basking in the sound of his rare laughter had made her cognizant of one thing.

She wanted to experience real kisses for once in her life, and if they were with this man, even better. Though he hadn't tried to steal one the night before nor had he acted untoward with her throughout the day, Hope couldn't dislodge the thought. Was it too much to ask of the universe that she experience desire or even passion before she consigned her life to being a companion?

Click!

The sound of the door snicking closed yanked her from her musings. Hope focused her gaze on the duke as he set about lighting one of the candles. Then he sank onto the side of the bed and removed his boots. Both of them fell to the worn hardwood floor with dual thuds.

How often would she see him since the elderly woman was his aunt? Would a few shared kisses between them make a proper relationship difficult? Perhaps it didn't matter. She would never trap him into marriage or even consent to become his mistress if he should ask.

"Are you certain you feel quite well?"

Once more, she startled. Shoving the thoughts quite firmly from her mind, Hope nodded. "I am fine. Please don't concern yourself."

He regarded her with speculation. "If you are certain?"

"I am." She quickly nodded and gave him a smile. Would it set him at ease?

"Very well." Brook removed his jacket then tossed it to the foot of the bed. "Let us hope the water has had a chance to thaw. I would like to at least attempt a shave tonight else I'll look a fright by the morning."

"Oh, I don't know. You look rather dashing right now." What would it feel like to drag her lips along the side of his jaw where the stubble ended, and the smooth skin began?

"Ah." A bit of a flush rose up his neck, visible when he removed his cravat. "I'm afraid I don't know what to say." His cuffs and collar followed the length of silk onto the end of the bed.

"Take the compliment." She waved him off. "I shall wash up once you're finished."

He removed the waistcoat. It hit the bed and then slid silently to the floor. "Thank you." After a few minutes of digging about his trunk, he took a small, rectangular-shaped, leather-bound box with him to the wash basin. While he was busy with ablutions that included shaving, washing his face, as well as brushing his teeth, Hope poked through the belongings in her own trunk. After a quick sniff of her traveling dress, she wrinkled her nose. Perhaps a dab or two of her precious violet perfume was in order. Once that was accomplished, she pulled out a small vanity set. Her hair could do with a good brushing, and each time she used the brush and mirror with the tortoiseshell handles, she remembered her mother, who'd given her the kit on her sixteenth birthday. By the time she'd gathered her supplies, the duke had finished with his nightly toilette. She nodded to him in passing and then ducked behind the privacy screen with a sigh of relief.

Good grief but the man was potent! Just being in the same cozy room with him had her heart pounding and her breath shallowing. His presence filled the space and practically demanded that she notice him. Well, how could she not? He was easily the most handsome man she'd seen in a long while, and he excited her on a level not even her fiancé had managed. That alone was cause for alarm, but she ignored the warning bells tolling in her head.

Tonight, she wouldn't rest until she'd had a kiss from him. It would keep her heated during the cold night ahead, for the wind still blew with gusto and the snow continued to fall. Lighter than last night, but a nuisance anyway.

When she came out from behind the screen in her shift, the duke was preparing a pallet on the floor, using his greatcoat for a bed.

Hope frowned. "You slept on the floor last night. I won't have you make that sacrifice again." Gently but with purpose, she took his arm and drew him away. Then she returned the pillow to the bed. "It is much too cold."

"But—"

"None of that, Your Grace." When he narrowed his gaze on her, she giggled. "Brook." With a giddy feeling of power and knowing he watched her, she made her way slowly around the bed. "Sharing is a necessity. Anything else is silly, and you are much too intelligent to act the nodcock."

His eyes glittered in the light from the candle nub as she crawled beneath the bedclothes. "Perhaps you are right. My limbs were nearly ice last night." Then he removed his shirt, and she stared, breathless at the expanse of his chest and its sprinkling of hair before he dropped the garment to the floor.

"I'm glad you have come to your senses." She smiled to herself. Did this smack too much of manipulation? She wasn't one of those fast women who wished to bed any man she came across merely to see who would become her next protector.

The bedclothes rustled and the bed depressed as the duke joined her. Oh, he smelled so good! Now was her chance. If she ever wanted to experience a kiss—and with a duke no less—there was no better time. Quickly scooting into the middle of the bed, Hope surged into him and pressed her lips to his. His warmth was addicting. He laid there in apparent shock as his eyes widened. The man did absolutely nothing to help the kiss along or even try to embrace her. Was he not interested, or had she truly surprised him?

"Oh, drat." Her stomach muscles knotted with anxiety. "Pardon my forwardness." The heat of mortification slapped her cheeks. She had made an unwanted advance toward a duke. Her reputation would be cut to ribbons if any of this were to find its way into the *ton*. With a half-stifled cry of embarrassment, Hope moved back to her side of the bed, and faced away from him, much as she'd done last night.

"What the devil is happening?" He cleared his throat. "Why did you do that?" Confusion was evident in his tone.

"Please forget that ever happened." Even to her own ears, the words were pathetic.

Remarkably, he chuckled. "Forget that a lovely, clever, talented woman kissed me? I think not."

Not even his praise could yank her out of the hole of awkwardness she'd fallen into. "Go to sleep, Your Grace."

"How many times have I asked you to make use of my name?" he asked in a soft voice.

She wiped at an escaped tear in the corner of her eye. "Go to sleep, *Brook*."

When he briefly touched her shoulder, she nearly vaulted off the bed at the charged energy that flowed through her. "Why did you kiss me, Hope?"

Obviously, he wouldn't leave her alone unless she explained. "I merely wished for a return of the closeness we had last night. It made me feel…" How much should she confess? Then, deciding in for a penny in for a pound, she continued, "…made me feel as if I'm not a failure in everything a woman of quality is supposed to excel at." Though the candor of the moment surprised her, a smidgeon of relief sailed down her spine.

At least the truth was finally out. Let him do with it what he would.

"If it is closeness you want, that can be had without kissing."

Oh, what a dear, clueless man he was. Hope snorted, for it was a little bit funny. "What if I *wanted* the kissing?" Was that too shocking to admit as well?

For long moments, the duke didn't respond, then he wrapped an arm about her waist, pulled her closer and encouraged her body to roll over until she faced him. "Why?" His intense blue gaze had the power to steal her breath. Could she drown in those eyes if she tried hard enough?

But he expected an answer. As best she could while lying on her left side, she shrugged. Heat burned in her cheeks. "I have never had the opportunity and I fear I never will now." Being under the thumb of an exacting elderly peeress meant her social life—such as it was—would grind to a halt.

One of Brook's blond eyebrows rose. "Your fiancé never kissed you?"

"Ha!" Though she wanted to laugh in self-derision, she frowned instead. It was difficult to concentrate with the duke so near and half naked. "Not in the way that put fire in my blood." A tiny sigh escaped. This next bit would make her appear ever more pathetic. "I have only known proper gentlemen, and they have never done anything else to me. As evidenced from my unwed, unwanted, undesired state. With the exception of some fumbling touches with my fiancé before... everything broke."

Oh, Hope, please stop talking!

Why did she tell him that? And apparently it wasn't enough, for an urge deep inside encouraged her to confess everything else currently troubling her soul. "And even though I orally pleasured my fiancé..." Finally, she gained control over her rambles with a gasp as she stared at him in horror. "Please forget I said that. Oh, please, please, please pretend I didn't," she implored in a small voice.

Why couldn't the bed crack in half and the floor swallow her up?

"Ah, Hope, you are such a refreshing breath of fresh air in this world." When Brook chuckled, the rich sound reverberated in her chest. "I take no offense in either word or deed, though both give me a little more background on you."

"Oh."

"And there is nothing wrong with wanting to exchange pleasure with the man to whom you were engaged. If someone tries to shame you for that, it shows their characters, not yours."

Another round of heat went through her cheeks. Never had she met a more understanding man. "I wanted to show him how I felt, give him something to remember me by when he returned to the field." She huffed with frustration. "Not that it mattered, since he begged off the engagement not two weeks later."

"Adding to what I have already said about the man, he was a nodcock." The duke tucked a lock of her hair that had escaped her braid behind her ear. "I am quite certain if you wished to make a match, you could find someone within society."

This time she did snort. "There won't be much cause to circulate through Yorkshire society unless your aunt enjoys that side of life, but you said she is rather exacting…"

"That's a nice way of putting it. I would say obnoxious." He chuckled. "Let us not discuss my aunt right now."

"All right." When she would have rolled back over, he stayed her with a hand on her shoulder. "Was there something else?

"Yes." Amusement twinkled in his eyes. "Truth be told, I *am* rather good at kissing, or so my wife always said." That little crooked grin held her spellbound.

"Do you miss it?" There was so much she didn't know about him.

"That closeness, that intimacy?" Emotions flit over his face she understood all too well. "I do, at times, and then I put those feelings away, go about my daily life. But they sneak back in, and the grief hits me again. At times, it's an endless loop without escape."

Tears again prickled the backs of her eyelids. "I know how you feel." Her chin quivered the longer she looked at him. "I miss my parents fiercely. Grief is always there, lurking, waiting to catch us unawares."

"Then the only answer is to learn to make room for it? Though I don't wish to lose those memories, I don't want to be held prisoner by them."

Hope nodded. "Making room is a good explanation. Those memories do not deserve to be forgotten, not by either of us, but they *are* in the past and we cannot live there. Whatever it holds, the future is where we might find happiness again."

"Sometimes I wonder if happiness is even possible for me after everything." For long moments, he peered into her eyes. "We have gotten rather off the topic of kissing, don't you think?"

"Perhaps." She gave him a small smile. "Your Grace—Brook—you have my promise I will not manipulate the situation or demand you marry me." It was important for him to understand that. She wanted nothing from him outside of this night. "I know where my life is headed. And we both understand it won't be as the wife of a titled gentleman. That was never my fate to begin with."

"I see." He stared at her as the guttering flame of the candle sent weird shapes dancing along the walls, the look in his eyes enigmatic. "Perhaps we can work within those parameters, then." Watching her the whole time, Brook slipped a hand around her nape and another on her hip. He pulled her close to his body, and then equally as slowly, even as she trembled, he claimed her lips with his.

Merciful heavens, I am being properly kissed by a duke!

It was as lovely as she'd hoped it would be.

His lips cradled hers as gently as his hand cradled the back of her head. For long moments, he moved his mouth over hers, allowing her to become acquainted with him, giving an introduction, telling her without words who he was and what sort of man she could expect.

Sensation shuddered down her spine, for in that one kiss there was a hidden promise. Of what she didn't know, wouldn't dare to think, but it was wonderful to see it glimmering there in the far recesses of her mind. Almost timidly, she mimicked what he did until she'd gotten the gist of how to not act like a cold fish. Then she slipped her hands up from where they rested on his bare chest to loop about the breadth of his shoulders. The duke moved slightly to settle her more comfortably in his embrace, and the strength of his arms around her was quite thrilling.

Then the pattern shifted, almost indiscernibly. Brook nibbled at the corners of her mouth, and then he lightly nipped at her bottom lip. Unexpected pleasure speared through her, zipped from her breasts to between her thighs.

"Ooh!" She stilled in an effort to make sense of the addition, and when he chuckled, a sea of sensation washed over her.

"If you are not comfortable with this, I shall beg off."

"Please, continue. It is... different." Hope pulled away just enough to peer into his eyes. "I had thought, stupidly, that kissing was merely the press of lips against each other." He had opened the door to so many other possibilities she didn't know what to do first.

"Oh, it is so much more than that." One of his eyebrows arched in question, and when she gave him a shy nod, he claimed her lips again.

This time the introductions were finished, and the mood of the embrace changed. The duke drew the tip of his tongue across the expanse of her bottom lip. Tingles went through her lower belly, for it was both naughty and sweet at the same time. He kissed her with such leisure, as if he had all the time in the world, that she was easily lost and did her best to return those kisses. Not that it was a chore, for she'd become addicted to the press of his body against hers, the slight taste of mint on his mouth, the softness of his hair as it glided through her fingers at his nape.

Then he encouraged her lips to part, and as confusion beset her, he touched the tip of his tongue to hers, and her world tilted again. Satin slid against silk, forcing her to learn a whole new style of kissing, but this was so much more erotic than she could ever dream.

Hope clung to him as she became unmoored from reality. The thrill of dueling with his tongue was a new experience for her. Excitement shivered up her spine, and with it came a longing for something she didn't quite understand.

Once more, the mood of the embrace shifted, and he returned to kissing her gently and leisurely without the deepness they'd just shared. She didn't care, for it was just as wonderful, and she couldn't wait to go through the whole gambit again. True to his word, the duke didn't push for anything beyond the joy of kissing even as the hard evidence of his desire pressed insistently against her hip.

For a long time, she was lost to exploring his lips, to dragging her lips beneath the sharp cut of his jaw, to letting her fingers drift down the length of his back. Brook did the same, and each pass, every feather-weighted kiss and nip under her jaw or tiny little lick he gave beneath her earlobe or on the side of her neck sent her tumbling toward a shimmering edge, of what she couldn't fathom.

Yet time and time again, she returned to his lips, and when the candle nub finally guttered out and the scent of smoke filled the air, Hope pulled away with a sigh of pure contentment.

"That was amazing," she whispered and was glad for the darkness crowding through the room, for her cheeks blazed with heat and her nipples ached with arousal, begging for his touch, and with it came a longing to fulfil her in ways a kiss never could.

"I am glad I could at least give you this."

"Did you enjoy it as well?"

"Surprisingly, yes, so thank you for that escape." He released her, and a bit of his warmth faded. "Goodnight, Hope. Sleep well."

"Goodnight, Brook." With a smile, she turned onto her other side and faced away from him. Minutes later, a wave of exhaustion fell over her. *I can become incredibly used to having the attentions of a man for no other reason than he wanted to kiss me.* For the first time in a long while, she didn't wrestle with worry over her future, and sleep wasn't elusive.

Chapter Eight

December 23, 1810
Middle of the night

Deborah, please don't go!

Brook came awake with a racing heart and a sense of unfathomable loss and loneliness. He shoved a hand through his hair then wiped a sheen of sweat from his brow. As he'd done with fair regularity since his wife had died, he'd dreamed of her again. The images had been so vivid, so real, and in this dream, he'd been kissing her, only the embrace didn't have the familiar feel it once did.

There had been an excitement there, a heat that was the same only different, and the scent of violets had haunted those dreams. Which had been odd.

Then the dream had shifted, and instead of Deborah beckoning him to be with her in the world beyond, she smiled at him and nodded, waved him away. What the hell did that mean?

Still, his heart ached, and he missed her to the point that he cried silently to himself in the dark. After a bit, his tears stopped, and he wiped the moisture from his cheeks. *Pull yourself together, Denton. It has been over two years.* While his mind knew this, his heart had trouble accepting the reality at times. As his heartbeat settled into a more normal rhythm, he watched the shadows play across the ceiling. The flying snow made interesting and eerie patterns on the window glass, for neither he nor Hope had closed the drapes.

Though the wind had slacked, flakes of snow floated across the glass. He turned his head to regard the woman sleeping next to him. During the night, she'd flopped onto her back with one arm flung over her shoulder on the pillow. The sound of her even breathing somehow brought him a queer sense of comfort to chase away the lingering anxiety and some of the grief the dreams had wrought.

After her request that he kiss her when they'd laid down for sleep, and she'd revealed more about her past with a heavy blush in her cheeks, he'd thought over her words with all seriousness. There was no denying there was a current of attraction bouncing between them, and though she had only wished for kissing, he was more experienced in such matters. Rarely did two people ever stop with that.

Yet, he had with Hope. It didn't matter that each time he was in close proximity with her — especially with their necessary sleeping arrangements — his shaft was all too interested in her. Knowing all of this, he'd kissed her anyway, and it had been such a wonderful experience that he'd willingly spent the next hour doing much of the same. He hadn't touched her in an overt, sexual manner, hadn't let the embrace go further than the kisses she'd asked for, but damn he'd wanted to explore her heated, rounded body that had been intimately pressed against his.

But would he betray Deborah's memory if he did?

"Brook?" Hope awakened, her voice rough with sleep. "Is something wrong?"

That inquiry of caring in the dark was both eerie and thrilling. It had been a long time indeed since a woman had done so, and damn if his shaft didn't harden. "All is well." His whisper sounded overly loud in the winter's silence.

"I thought I heard you crying." When he didn't answer, she rolled onto her side to face him, and the warmth of her was all too tempting. "Why are you upset?"

"Honestly, I don't wish to talk about it." For that would only make him want to bury himself into her honeyed heat if only to forget for a moment that he was alone.

"Come now, Your Grace." Hope wriggled closer. She laid a palm on his chest, and he gasped from the unexpected delight of that touch. "You have made me talk about things I didn't wish to. Now I shall listen to you. Perhaps then you won't suffer so acutely once night falls."

"I have a tendency to dream about my wife," he said in a low voice but doubted that talking about Deborah would have any sort of affect except making his grief flare.

"Perhaps that is the only way you know how to work through your feelings, but surely you must know she would understand if you wished to move past them."

Did he want to? Would that mean she would disappear from his mind? There were no easy answers, but since both he and Hope were awake, where was the harm in talking about some of what troubled him. "I never thought I would adore being married, but I did."

"That is so lovely to hear a man say. Usually, they complain about the wedded state or would rather brag on the mistresses they took." The respect in her voice was obvious and made him grin slightly.

"Well, I did, and I never took a mistress. Deborah was enough."

She drifted her hand down his bare arm, leaving awareness tingling in her wake. "How long were you with her?"

"Married? Nearly six years, but I had courted her for six months and we enjoyed an engagement of another six months."

"Ah." The almost rhythmic stroking of her fingers made him relax by increments. "Then can I assume she was young when you met?"

He chuckled into the darkness. Not able to see her expression or the emotions in her eyes all that clearly due to the gloom, Brook concentrated on the outline of her form. "To be honest, my family and hers had been around each other since I was in the cradle. I was just a lad when Deborah was born; the first child of an earl. Their properties bordered ours."

"Did your fathers expect you would marry?"

"I suppose so, but I'd violently opposed that idea, for being a boy, I wanted nothing to do with all of that." He shrugged. "However, as the years marched on and I went away to school, I'd forgotten all about her. After my Grand Tour, I came back to London to see about amassing a fortune of my own without my father's help, and I met Deborah again at a ball. She was eighteen and clearly a Diamond of the First Water in her Come Out year."

"It was her first Season?"

"Quite, and she was the typical girl straight out of the schoolroom." Another chuckle escaped him. "I was immediately enamored of her, smitten from the first."

"She didn't mind the age gap?"

"Of course not. Such things don't matter within the *beau monde*."

Hope snickered. "Careful, Your Grace. Your privilege is showing."

He rather liked the fact this bit of womanhood acted as a moral compass at times. "Yes, well, it is difficult to remember. Suffice it to say, I married Deborah, and we began our lives together in short order." Words tumbled through his mind, falling over each other, all clamoring to be heard. "She had been everything proper a woman raised in the *ton* and the daughter of an earl could be—demure, unexcitable, perfect in every way. She was proficient in needlework, watercolor painting, and the pianoforte."

A huff escaped Hope, and the warmth of it skated across his throat. "That only means she was like every other lady in society. What did you like about her alone?"

No one had asked that before, and he'd never needed to examine the subject. Heat crept up the back of his neck. "I'm embarrassed to say I don't know. I admired all of those things about her, and she was beautiful besides. I guess I assumed that was what I should have looked for in a wife." Perhaps that had been wrong, for when he compared Deborah to Hope, they were as different as night and day. He rather doubted Hope was the demure and retiring sort, and she was certainly outspoken and daring. All things Deborah never was. "We were from the same world with the same viewpoints, and we were both excited to start a nursery."

As if that were an excuse.

"That is to be expected from a couple in love." She glided her fingers over his chest, down his ribcage, then over his hip in an enticing, meandering path that served as both a distraction and ushered in heightened awareness until his shaft throbbed with need. "Obviously, the two of you were compatible in every way, since you miss her so fiercely."

"Perhaps." While he'd enjoyed bedding Deborah, it had become a bit of a chore, for she wasn't one to initiate couplings and neither was she adventurous. She was… proper even in that. Had the whole of his life been based in the wrong things? He had followed all the rules, done what was expected of a man in his position, went according to a plan. "I, uh, hadn't been a duke yet, so we were afforded a bit more freedom."

"What? No scandals to be had?" The teasing in her voice went straight to his stones.

"Perish the thought." Unlike his sudden relationship with Hope, which had been nothing but scandal from the first. His chuckle sounded all too forced even to his ears. "Five years into my marriage, I was handed the dukedom." Need shivered down his spine, for all he could concentrate on was the caress of her fingers over his skin. What would it feel like if she were to curl those digits around his shaft? *Oh, God! Stop thinking, Denton!* "Father died of an aggressive cancer of some sort. It took him quickly. We were all stunned by the illness."

"I'm sorry for your loss. When my parents died, I was lost and inconsolable for months following the event."

Which he would ask her about at a later time. "I didn't have much time to mourn. Mother died shortly after of what I suspect was a broken heart. Then Deborah told me she was increasing. I thought my life had turned and that fortune was with me." Knowing he would soon be a father himself had taken some of the sting from losing his parents and having to square with the responsibilities of being a duke. Memories of that time crashed into each other to form a veritable storm in his chest, full of all that pain and sorrow of the time.

"You have had quite the time of it." Her whisper soothed the worst of the anguish, and he marveled at that fact. "What happened to the pregnancy?"

He swallowed hard past the lump of emotion in his throat. "The babe came too soon. Two months early, in fact. Neither of us knew what to do, and time was of the essence. There were complications with the birth I have long forgotten the explanations of." His words came too fast; grief graveled his voice. "There was so much blood, Hope." He found her gaze in the darkness, willed her to understand. "By the time a midwife came to the house, it was much too late to save either Deborah or the babe." With a tightness in his chest and grief exploding around him, Brook slipped an arm about Hope's waist and drew her closer to his body.

Was it odd that being with her made him feel less alone or without purpose?

"That must have been a terrible time for you." She stilled her fingers on his shoulder. The glitter of her eyes in the darkness comforted him. "Will you marry again?"

"For the responsibilities to my title? Probably."

"No, Brook, that is not what I meant." Hope brushed the hair from his forehead with an angel-like touch. "I mean for *you*. Would you let yourself fall in love again?"

Of course, there was a difference. Why hadn't he seen it before? "I don't know. It is much to ask of my heart and my head. There are times when I can barely withstand the grief now, and it's been over two years. Love hurts too much for me to consider it again."

Was that true, though?

"Because you won't give yourself room to grow or consider the possibility that you can have happiness again, but your reticence is understandable." She briefly cupped his cheek before gliding her hand back to his shoulder. "Begging your pardon, but I believe such thinking is flawed."

"What do you mean?"

"When someone's heart is broken, they always say that love hurts-, but I stand by my argument. Based on my own experience and from what I've seen of the world, that is."

He frowned. "Please explain." There was something about this woman who encouraged him to look at everything differently. She shattered his preconceived notions, and he was beginning to crave that more and more.

"Well, consider this. Loneliness hurts. Rejection hurts. Loss hurts. Envy hurts. As does jealousy. Perhaps many people confuse all of those emotions with love, but truly, love is the *only* thing in this confusing world that blankets the pain and makes a person feel... wonderful." She shrugged and her fingers stilled. "And that is why I believe, deep down in my soul, love is the only thing we as humans should chase. The rest of those feelings don't matter. They don't heal as love does."

"You are a marvel, do you know that? Even as hurt as you have been, you can manage to offer a philosophical insight that completely changes everything I've ever known about myself or the world." She didn't answer, and he didn't push. For long moments, he held her close, borrowed from her strength, basked in the warmth of her. There wasn't the feeling of being so scattered or tangled now he'd talked about his history, and he marveled over that. Would she let him to do the same for her? "Thank you for tonight. It has helped, this not being alone, this beginning to let go of those memories and give them to someone else so I don't need to carry them alone."

"You are welcome." He felt her smile more than saw it. "For the first time in many months, I'm glad to be of use to someone. It is much different than *being* used by someone."

"I suppose it is." Was that how she'd seen her life up until this point? How terribly sad. Hope was a wonderful, caring person who didn't deserve to be treated with less than respect.

"May I tell you a secret?"

"Of course." Brook slipped a hand down her back and paused at the dip at the base of her spine. Oh, she felt so good in his arms!

"I detest being in mourning. It is quite dull."

"On that, I agree with you." They shared a chuckle, and in that moment, the air between them became charged again. In talking with her, he'd temporarily forgotten the raw lust and desire that had steadily grown between them. Now it came roaring back, demanded attention. Beyond that, the woman he held was a breath of fresh air he didn't realize he'd needed. "Ah,

Hope, I am exceedingly glad to have been stranded in a storm with you. It has made such a difference." Then, before he could change his mind, he sought out her lips, ultimately claimed them in a gentle kiss that left him craving so much more.

"Brook, I…" For whatever reason, she didn't finish her thought, but her lips brushed his with both of those words.

"Shh." How much did he want this woman? It was insanity, though, and he refused to take advantage, for she was no doubt an innocent and didn't deserve such depraved treatment that meant absolutely nothing except relieving frustrated sexual tension. Again, he kissed her, wished that would be enough.

But the unrelenting drive to join with her wouldn't fade.

"I have always wanted to know what being appreciated felt like. Now I know. It is much better than being rejected for my looks." There was such wonder in her tone that his chest tightened for a completely different reason.

"It is, of course, gammon as I've said before." Daring much, he took her hand and put it against his erection with a groan. "If ever you assume you are not a woman who can inspire a man to passion, remember what *this* feels like. And this has nothing to do with your looks."

"That is *quite* an impression, Your Grace, and it leaves me in awe. And it demands attention." Before he could form words—for merely having her hand against his member taxed his control—Hope plucked the buttons of his frontfalls from their holes. One by one, and then she drew the panel of his breeches open, and his engorged length sprang free.

"What are you doing? Need graveled his voice. Surely this was wrong.

"Giving you comfort and a distraction from grief." She found his gaze in the dark, and when he attempted to swat her hand away, she giggled. "In this, I know what to do."

"But—"

"Shh. You gave me the same earlier tonight by indulging my fantasy for kissing." When she drew a fingertip up and down his straining shaft, he nearly jumped off the bed. "Let me do the same for you. Because I can. Because you need the release."

He tried once more. "It is not proper." Brook tugged her hand away even though the whole of his being wanted to feel her fingers on him, needed that carnal connection.

"As you told me when we came to bed tonight, nothing we have done this trip has been proper." She giggled and the lighthearted sound went straight to his stones. "Consider it a gift, Mr. Gerard."

Bloody hell. What a coil.

Apparently, she took his silence for acquiescence, for she sat up and threw off the bedclothes. With what he assumed was the devil's own grin, the woman kneeled at his side, wrapped her delicate fingers around his shaft and then began to stroke her hand up and down.

"Dear God." The touch was both heaven and hell. Naturally, he spread his legs even as his mind screamed a warning, told him to dissuade her.

"My fiancé taught me how to pleasure him with my mouth, and I hope I do this correctly on you." She rested her free hand on his abdomen, and the muscles in his stomach clenched. "If so, it was only thing of value he ever gave me." Faint bitterness had entered her voice. "For it certainly wasn't his heart or his name."

There would be time enough to delve into her secrets, but for now, the only thing his mind could comprehend was the squeeze and release of her hand on his shaft.

Did she realize she hummed a tuneless song as she worked? It was both curious and arousing. His member tightened further until his could hardly withstand the urge to throw her backward onto the bed for no other purpose except to bury himself deep.

"No wonder your wife was so satisfied by you," she whispered as she drew her curled fingers up and down. Then she twisted and began the torture all over again. "Any woman would be." As he fisted the bedclothes in a hand,

Hope caressed her fingers along the inside of his thighs, but the relief of having her leave off his member was short-lived, for she gently cupped his stones, giggling when he sucked in a shocked breath.

"Deborah considered it the height of scandal to manipulate my equipage," he managed to gasp out and renewed his grip on the sheet.

"I'm sorry to hear that. She missed out on a lovely way to bring her husband pleasure that didn't involve being bedded." When he thought she might have finished her exquisite torture, she managed to shock him again by bending over him. One second her lips hovered over the head of his shaft, her breath warming the tip, and the next, she took that point between those two pieces of flesh and lightly suckled.

"Damn!" The hiss sounded overly loud in the silence of the room.

Hope's only response was a chuckle moments before she went down and took most of his erection into the warm cavern of her mouth. With a hand still resting on his abdomen and her other continuing to stroke the base of his shaft or lightly squeeze his stones, she bobbed up and down. When she wasn't eating the length of him, she nibbled and licked every centimeter of its surface, and apparently enjoyed the act. With each varied movement, the need to spend grew more urgent.

He gritted his teeth. Heaven and hell, night and day. The woman bringing him to the brink of pleasure was as different from his wife as that, and it was a startling change. Eventually, she found a rhythm she enjoyed, and there was nothing to do but revel in the hot glide of her lips and tongue along his member. Both wanting the erotic torture to end and have it never finish, Brook put a hand to her head, wrapped her brown braid around his palm in order to guide her attentions to where he needed her to be.

Not able to withstand the sensations crashing over him, he thrust upward into the bliss that was her mouth, going as deep as he dared until his tip hit the back of her throat. A murmured sound escaped her, but as he watched, she didn't act as if she protested, so he withdrew slightly only to stroke into her mouth again. Each time he did, she squeezed his stones, but the moment she stroked two fingers over the sensitive skin between them and his arse, a rush of pure, raw pleasure slammed into him and sent him hurtling toward that glimmering edge.

"Hope! Dear God, what are you doing to me?" Nothing like this had ever happened between him and Deborah, and though he'd taken himself in hand more than a few times since his wife had died, the end result was nothing like this.

The very wickedness, the feeling of wonder, of belonging that pulsed through his body took him by surprise and threw him well past the point of no return.

"I cannot hold back." Refusing to spend down her throat, for that was a vulgar display at best, Brook uttered a strangled cry that the neighbor who shared a wall no doubt heard. He'd barely urged her off him and swung his legs over the side of the bed before an incredible pulse of release roared through his shaft. He came hard and with such force it splattered onto the floor and against the wall. "Damnation, woman, that was incredible." The manhood in his hand continued to jerk and pulse, and by the time he was empty, exhaustion crept in around the edges.

"Isn't that the point of such exercise?" she asked softly as the bedclothes rustled.

For long moments, Brook willed his breathing to return to normal. "That wasn't well done of me, and a rather ugly display no lady should have to see." Heat crept up the back of his neck, for it was rare he lost control as he'd done just now.

Her giggle was much like a balm to his ragged nerves. "We all have needs and feelings." She touched a hand to his back, and damn if his fickle shaft didn't twitch with a modicum of renewed interest. "That is how we know we're still alive."

"Perhaps." Daring to glance over his shoulder as she came near on her knees, he shivered. "Thank you all the same."

"You are quite welcome." As she bussed his cheek, her breast brushed against his arm, and there was no mistaking the hardened tip of her nipple. Had the act aroused her as well? "Now you won't see being with another woman as a hurdle to overcome. It should be easier for you to court a lady."

"I wonder."

She patted his shoulder. "Goodnight, Brook. I hope you suffer no further nightmares."

"So do I." As she nestled into the bed and brought the counterpane over her body, he stood, rooted about the contents of his trunk for a clean handkerchief, and then began the task of cleaning up the mess the best he could.

One thing was certain. Looking at her over the breakfast table in the morning would be the height of awkward. Was there a certain protocol for interacting with a woman after she'd sucked him off? To say nothing of how that innocent kiss to his cheek had made him feel beyond comforted.

What the devil am I to do now?

Chapter Nine

December 23, 1810
Morning

Hope came awake gradually, and when she opened her eyes fully, it was to the most welcome sight. Weak sunlight came through the window since the curtains hadn't been drawn the night before, and she blinked from the unexpected illumination. Clouds scudded across the skies, but they were breaking, and the valiant sun would have its victory, perhaps by noon.

Flutters of excitement went up her spine. The storm was over!

As she watched, snow no longer danced past the window glass and neither did the sound of the wind whistle around the panes. At long last, the work of digging out the roads would begin and if the temperatures continued to climb, perhaps some of the snow would melt.

Then her spirits plummeted, and knots of worry pulled in her belly.

Oh, no! The storm is over.

That meant her time alone with the duke was nearly at an end. With a frown, Hope rolled over. Brook remained in slumber beside her, but unlike the two nights they'd already spent, there was no longer much distance between them on the bed. In fact, he laid in repose not six inches away. Her heart trembled. Unexpectedly, they had become bonded together, but now the snow and wind had subsided, how long would it be before their little charade was done and they would be forced to move on to Yorkshire where he would give her into his aunt's care?

There was simply no way to tell.

The even rise and fall of the duke's chest recalled her attention. She planted her elbow onto the bed and propped her chin into her hand while she observed him. Truly, he was a beautiful man. A faint shadow of stubble had crept over his jaw, chin, and cheeks. Blond hair mixed with threads of silver, which matched the hair on his head and chest. There was a faint smile flirting with his lips while he slept, and she hoped his dreams were sweet. Beyond his physical attributes—some of which she'd been more than intimately acquainted with the night before—his soul was lovely. During their time together, he'd been receptive to new ideas and eager to change his thinking.

Both would let him go far as he continued his work in parliament or in the event he wished to enter into the Marriage Mart again. Worry knotted in her belly once more. Even though a shaft of jealousy speared through her, she pushed it away. Of course, he wasn't for her — they didn't move in the same circles — but she wished him well in the pursuit of happiness and perhaps finding love anew. He wasn't the sort of man to spend the remainder of his life alone. A good woman would only enhance who he was.

Never would she regret the time she had been given with him this Christmastide. He had shown her what it was like to be wanted and desired even if they hadn't coupled, and never would he know how much that meant to her. She would long dine out on the memories created with him while she slept in her lonely bed in Yorkshire.

On impulse, Hope leaned over him and brushed his lips with hers. "I hope you find whatever it is you are searching for, Brook." Her whispered words sounded too loud in the stillness of the morning. "Above all, I pray you let happiness enter your life again if it presents itself." When tears prickled the backs of her eyelids, she maneuvered from the bed as quietly as she could without waking him.

Quickly padding to the window, she peered outside. In the weak sunlight, the snow cover sparkled like millions of diamonds had fallen from the heavens. At least a foot of whiteness blanketed the ground. Drifts and hillocks dotted the landscape, but the precipitation had ceased. Sooner or later, the roads would be passable, though it was doubtful that would happen in the next couple of days.

Perhaps she shouldn't complain, for she would have a bit more time to pretend she was married to the man in the bed. With a smile, she made her way around the bed as the cold seeped into her bare feet.

As much as she tried to ignore thoughts of the duke as she made use of the chamber pot behind the privacy screen, he forced his way into her imagination anyway. In the clear light of morning, she was abashed at her daring from the night before. Good heavens, after talking to him and sharing all of those kisses with the man, she'd sought to bring him comfort and a distraction. Because of that, she'd taken his member into her mouth. She'd orally pleasured a duke, for Jove's sake! The fact that she'd trespassed so intimately, had done scandalous things to him sent heat into her cheeks. He'd even tried to dissuade her, but she'd done the deed anyway.

Thank goodness for his wherewithal not to spend down her throat. The courtesy was appreciated, but there had been a part of her that had wanted that honor, had wanted to taste him, to be the woman to leave such an impression upon him. What would have happened had he pulled her off him but instead of releasing his seed onto the floor, he'd claimed her body instead?

Oh, it is maddening to think about! And yet, there was a heavy sense of longing sitting inside because she wanted something she could never have.

More confused than ever, Hope washed her face and hands in the icy cold water. It had frozen around the edges but at least she could actually use the water this morning as opposed to yesterday. The bracing temperature of her abbreviated bath served to wake her fully and render her brain more alert. When her stomach released a resounding growl of hunger, she snickered. Never had she been hungrier than she had on this trip.

By the time she returned to the bed, the duke was awake, and he was watching her from his position of being propped against both pillows. The intense look in his eyes sent tingles of excitement down her spine to lodge between her thighs. "Good morning." The deep rumble tickled through her lower belly. "I trust you slept well."

"I did." It was wildly unfair that he appeared so refreshed and devilishly handsome without having done anything in the way of a toilet. "Did you?"

"Remarkably, yes. I cannot remember the last time I had no dreams—bad or otherwise."

"Perhaps you needed the uninterrupted rest."

"Perhaps." With casual elegance and leisure, he drifted his gaze up and down her body. "Thank you for last night. All of it. I, uh, appreciate what you did for me."

Was it her imagination or was the section of sheet draped over his lap tenting? Knowing he might be aroused by her again tugged a smile from her. "We all deserve a surcease from grief, Brook, all deserve to know there might be hope."

"Indeed." He grinned. "Hope." The corners of his eyes crinkled, and that look was devastating to her peace of mind. "You *are* hope, did you know that?"

Was he… flirting with her? Heat slapped at her cheeks. "I like to give that to others. Perhaps my parents named me correctly."

"I'll wager there's a story behind your name, hmm?"

"A bit."

"Will you tell me?"

"That depends." Her stomach released another definitive growl.

"On whether you have breakfast?" he asked with another grin.

"Yes." Oh, why was it so easy to talk to him? And why couldn't she stop staring at his naked chest? Or thinking that it might be fun to lap spilled tea from that flat abdomen?

"Very well." He nodded. "Shall I order breakfast, or do you wish to go down?"

Was it possible to expire from heat? Seeing him in such a state of undress in the daylight was rapidly diminishing her ability to think clearly. Touching that chest in the privacy of the darkness was one thing but being presented with the undeniable truth of his masculinity without shadow was quite another. "Uh…" She forced a swallow into her suddenly dry throat. "Honestly, I would rather eat here in this room, with you."

Would he think her a ninny? A bumpkin not fit to converse properly with a duke?

"Then I shall make it happen." Amusement twinkled in his blue eyes. "Though the storm has blown itself out, I'll venture to guess we will not leave this inn anytime soon."

From your lips to God's ears. And heaven help her to have the strength to leave him when that time *did* come. It had been all too lovely having a man pay such specialized attention to her.

Brook finished with a simple knot of his cravat in some bemusement, for behind the privacy screen, Hope was dressing, and she was all too excited about the prospect of breakfast. It was such a simple thing, but she apparently considered it a wonderful part of her day.

And perhaps she had the right of it. When he reached for his jacket—a rich brown superfine today merely to break the monotony of wearing the same thing—he glanced toward the screen. The prospect of dining with her in the privacy of their room was all too charming.

How was it possible a woman he'd met two days ago was making such an impression on him? It was maddening, or perhaps he was slowly going insane due to a Christmastide storm, but as she approached the bed, her smile lit the room, and he thought things wouldn't be half bad if he could wake up and see that for a handful of years more.

"The navy dress suits you." Cut more whimsically than her traveling outfit, the bodice was lower and gave a glimpse at the tops of her modest breasts, and it featured three-quarter sleeves. A faint trim of a satin ribbon, also in navy, went about the bottom hem of the dress.

"Thank you. I'm afraid my wardrobe is quite dull compared to what you are accustomed to seeing on ladies in London." She plucked an ivory woolen shawl from the bed and then wrapped it about her shoulders, which hid that tantalizing peek at her décolletage from view.

"Pish posh, Mrs. Gerard. You would look lovely in anything you don." *Or sans clothing if you would prefer.* Damnation, but how much did he want to see her naked and reclining on that bed for his consumption and perusal? His mind jogged to what she'd done to him last night, what he'd let her do, and heat twisted up his spine. He shouldn't have indulged, shouldn't have agreed, but the moment her warm, wet mouth had closed over his shaft, he'd been lost.

A pretty blush stained her cheeks. "You are too kind."

I am a man who hasn't been physical with a woman in far too long. And perhaps he was slowly going insane because of it. "No. I am honest." He struggled into the jacket, for if he asked for her assistance, he was afraid that her touch during an ordinary act such as putting said garment on might push him further into temptation.

Once more, he retreated into musings. Perhaps his earlier thought was ridiculous, but the longer he spent in her company, the more he came to admire and appreciate her. Life didn't work like that, and not between two people so far apart on society's scale. Hell, he'd courted his wife for six months before their engagement, and then was engaged for another six after that. Yet Hope, that bit of womanhood with bewitching features and a sense of fun, made him think he'd known her for a long time, and that if she were with him a few more days, she might give him a new purpose.

Was that what he wanted?

There was no way of knowing. Perhaps she merely had an old soul or perhaps it was fate that had put them here at the same time and it was just happenstance. Nothing more, but then how to explain the near-instant attraction and the scandal there were already mired in?

He didn't want to think too much about it, so he quickly did up the buttons while Hope shoved pins into her hair, securing the nondescript knot once more to the back of her head.

A discreet knock at the door interrupted any chance for further conversation, and as he swung the panel open, a modicum of relief shivered down his spine. At least right now he wouldn't act on the urge to claim her body. He gave a tight smile to the footman in the narrow corridor beyond.

"Your tea and breakfast, Mr. Gerard."

"Excellent." Brook stood aside and let the other man into the room. "Uh, has there been a report upon the state of the roads?"

The footman shook his head. "Not yet, but a few of us will go out after breakfast to make an assessment." He set a tray onto the top of the bureau. A teapot, two cups, and various assorted breakfast foods waited for consumption. "By teatime, we should have a few answers."

"Thank you." Brook closed the door once the footman departed. When he turned around, he caught Hope's gaze with his. She watched him with a certain wary sadness lining her face. "What?"

"I had acclimated myself—"

"—resigned yourself, you mean?" he interrupted with a grin merely to cheer her up.

"Fine." She sighed, and when her kissable lips curved with a tiny smile, his chest tightened. "Resigned myself to being stranded here for a week, but now that we might be on the road again so soon..."

He nodded as her words trailed off. "I understand. This has been an unexpected but lovely reprieve from day-to-day life." Cold dread twisted down his spine. Once the roads were passable and he delivered her to his aunt, their paths would separate. He was a duke, and she was in reduced circumstances, forced to take a position. It was highly unlikely they would ever meet again unless he traveled north again to visit his aunt.

Damn, that is a depressing thought.

"Yes." Her smile widened, and immediately his mood lifted. "It was something not anticipated but I'm glad it happened, if only for the opportunity to meet you."

Oh, God!

For the space of a few heartbeats, warmth spread around his heart. He experienced a sensation of incredible belonging, then he tamped it before such things could grow out of hand. "I could say the same of you." If he didn't gain control of his emotions, he would make a fool of himself. "Now, come, let us partake of this breakfast."

His hand shook as he poured out tea for her. The sense of dread persisted, though. His aunt would wear Hope down, would harangue her within an inch of her life, and surely dim her spark. How could he allow that to happen? But conversely, how could it not? This was her future, and if she didn't take this position, what would become of her? Brook stared too intently at her while she took her cup and frowned. If she didn't go forward, would she be forced to make a living on her back like what happened to so many other women in her circumstances?

Absolutely not. I won't allow it. Surely if she begged off this assignment, he could help in locating a different one, perhaps have her placed in London with a prominent family so he would have a chance to see her in society…

"Brook?"

"Yes?" He scowled at the teapot as he poured a measure into his own cup.

"What must your thoughts be to put such a fierce expression on your face?"

Heat crept up the back of his neck. "I apologize. Woolgathering, I suppose."

"Do you want to talk about it?" She joined him at the bureau and plucked one of the loaded plates from the tray. "I'm a good listener." When she bumped her hip against his, charged reaction streaked through him.

"Uh…" He took a gulp of the tea. It burned his throat and resulted in a bout of coughing. "It is nothing of consequence," he managed to gasp out as he wiped at his streaming eyes.

"All right." Hope took her plate over to the high-backed wooden chair. Once she sat down, she balanced the plate on her lap. "Perhaps later we could venture outside?"

"Whyever for?" The piece of toast he'd taken from his own plate remained uneaten in his hand as he paused. "It's snow." Truly, he was perplexed by her request.

"Yes, but it has been an age since we have had this much snow at Christmastide. I thought it might be fun to explore while the world has a blanket of white." A dreamy look fell over her. "Can you imagine what it would feel like to tramp through those woods?" She put her plate on the small table nearby next to her teacup and then moved to the window. "See there, Brook? There's a fox out foraging for a meal. That's a good indication the storm is well and truly over. Soon, the snow will begin to melt, I'll wager, and England will see a return of the rain. All the magic will be gone."

When she glanced at him from over her shoulder with that bewitching light in her doe-brown eyes and her features arrested in anticipation, a shudder went down his spine. The last thing he wished to do was go out into that fluffy cold world, but with a handful of words, she'd captivated him. How the devil did he think he could deny her anything?

"I would enjoy that." Perhaps a little too much. "We shall set out once we're finished with breakfast. Afterward, we will spend a bit of time in the common room with our fellow travelers and see how they're faring."

Because he would need the distraction. The more he was alone with Hope, the greater the urge to do something beyond scandalous to her—with her. The two of them could only be so lucky before someone discovered his true identity. Yet…

Hope giggled and once more her smile lit up the room. "Oh, this will be such fun, Your Grace." She laid a palm against the glass. "I haven't played in the snow since early in my childhood."

"Then we shall make certain today is something you'll never forget." *For I certainly won't.* His heart squeezed as he turned back to his breakfast. Already, he was being pulled forward, back into the land of the living to put distance between him and the heartbreak of the past. How had she managed to do that? He didn't know, but part of him was anxious to see what happened next.

Even if it meant their eventual parting would prove bittersweet.

Chapter Ten

"Where are you headed, Mrs. Gerard, looking like a winter fairy?"

Hope spun about at the sound of the innkeeper's voice as she stood by the door before moving outside. Though she'd donned the pelisse from her traveling outfit, she'd also pulled out a cloak of bright red. It was one of the most cheerful garments she owned, and it seemed festive enough for the occasion.

"Ah, Mr. Addams. Hello." Giving him a smile she hoped conveyed confidence, she shrugged. "I'm going outside to tramp through the snow. Don't you think it looks so inviting with sunlight sparkling upon it like a thousand diamonds?"

"It is pretty, I'll give you that." He glanced about the room. "Is Mr. Gerard going out with you?"

"He is."

They both turned as Brook approached. She sent him a grin, and when he returned the gesture, flutters filled her belly. "As my husband said, he has promised to accompany me, so there is no risk I'll be lost or stuck." While it was perfectly lovely to find herself stranded in an inn with the duke, being lost outside in the snow for several hours did not sound like an enjoyable adventure.

The innkeeper bounced his gaze between them both. "When you come back, sit near the fire. You'll probably be frozen to the bone." He shook his head. "Why anyone would want to be out there in the cold is beyond me."

"We won't be long but thank you for the concern. It is all so novel, this much snow." Brook slipped a hand around her upper arm and guided her over the floor toward the front door. Once they'd exited the common room and were away from a few curious looks, the duke grinned again, and this time the delicate skin at the corners of his eyes crinkled. "You are quite fetching in that cloak, Mrs. Gerard."

Heat sneaked into her cheeks. "It is warmer than the pelisse, and I figured if I did become lost, the red was striking enough against the snow that you could easily find me."

His fingers tightened slightly on her arm. "I would never allow you to wander that far from me in any event."

A path had been carved out from the door that ran around the side of the building toward the stables and another that branched in the rear so that firewood and other supplies could be taken inside… and no doubt refuse put out. She wasn't quite certain of the inner workings of an inn, but such things would have to be considered. Gauging by the wall of the shoveled snow, there must be at least eight inches on the ground. Stable hands were out using whatever tools they could find that would lift or push the snow from various areas of the ground.

"The world looks so pretty and incredible just now," Hope breathed with a fair amount of awe in her voice. "Doesn't it seem peaceful?"

"Indeed, almost like a hymn." He glanced at her with one eyebrow cocked beneath the brim of his beaver felt top hat. "Are you ready to leave the path? The snow might dampen your skirts and sneak over your boots."

"I am willing to risk that, for how often are we treated to such a magical world?" Forgetting everything except the need to experience what that large amount of snow felt like, she tugged on his hand and urged him off the path.

The going was slow, for the snow was heavy and it sucked at her feet a bit, much as if she were walking through mud. Each time she stumbled, Hope squealed and clung to his hand. It helped that he met with a bit of resistance in walking through the snow as well. Her skirts hampered movement, so throwing caution to the wind, she released his hand in order to hike that fabric up and out of the way. Cold snow crept into her boots, and that made her squeal too.

Soon enough, they passed into the wooded area. In spots, the snow wasn't as deep, and in others, it had drifted due to the winds from the storm. There was an ethereal hush through the barren trees and shrubberies. Here and there, bright red berries that clung heroically to the brambles provided a pretty pop of color. Wintertime birds flitted to and fro in the desperate search for food that wasn't buried. She explored as best she could, and only when the duke called her name did Hope turnabout.

That's when a ball of snow splattered against her chest. Cold flakes of the packed precipitation flew into her face and clung to her lips. Brook's laughter rang out in the silence.

"What was that for?" She brushed at the snow and then readjusted the hood of the cloak upon her head.

"No reason other than it was fun." Mischief twinkled in his eyes. "Do you wish to receive another?"

"Only if you want me to retaliate. It's no good teasing if you cannot have some of the same, Your Grace."

"Oh, we shall see about that." Already, he bent, scooped up more snow, and was forming a tidy ball.

She squealed when he lobbed his makeshift artillery, but she quickly threw one of her own that caught him on the shoulder and exploded upon impact. His expression of sheer astonishment made her laugh as if she hadn't a care in the world, and all too soon they threw snowballs back and forth until her hands were cold and she could no longer feel her toes.

"Are you declaring defeat, Mrs. Gerard?" he shouted with his hands propped on his hips. With his greatcoat and top hot, he seemed for all the world like a man lost in Hyde Park instead of a secretive duke snowbound at an inn.

"Only if you can catch me," she hollered back and then turned tail and ran as best she could through the snow, deeper into the woods.

"Minx!" The crunch of snow told her he'd given chase.

Giggling, Hope continued forward, but the toe of her boot caught in a root hidden beneath the snow. She stumbled and then fell into the soft whiteness, landing first on her side. It felt so good and so lovely that she flopped onto her back if only to luxuriate in it.

"Hope, are you harmed?" Concern sound in the duke's voice as he dropped to his knees beside her.

"I have never been so well!" Wanting him to experience the same thing, she sprang at him, but her skirts impeded movement. She tumbled headlong into his body, knocking him askew and when he flounced onto his back, she sprawled over his chest. That pulled another giggle from her throat. "This has been such a lovely morning." Scrambling into a sitting position, she straddled his waist. Thank goodness they were far enough into the tree line that they wouldn't be readily seen from the inn... unless someone peered out an upstairs window.

He ran his gloved hands up her legs to rest on either side of her waist. "Yes, it has." Gone was the mischief from his sapphire eyes, replaced by a certain wicked promise that had the power to steal her breath.

"Thank you for accompanying me." As she gazed down at him, noted his top hat a few feet from him, admired the contrast of his somber coat against the brilliant whiteness of the snow, realized the solid hardness of his body beneath hers, awareness tingled over her. "For that matter, thank you for the past few days. I have wildly enjoyed this experience."

"So have I." The duke tugged at the side of her cloak, brushed snow from her cheek with equally snow-encrusted fingers of his gloves. "Never will I forget how you look right now in this moment, with that red cloak and the blush of cold in your cheeks and with delight in your eyes." He shook his head. "Your former fiancé was a damned fool," he whispered seconds before he yanked her down over him and he crushed his lips to hers.

Oh, such heaven on Earth! The warmth of his lips coupled with the possessive slide of his hand down her spine to the curve of her bottom had tiny fires igniting through her blood. Where she'd thought tramping through the snow and throwing balls at him had been the height of fun, there was simply nothing in the world as wonderful as kissing a duke in a world glittering with cold diamonds.

Only now, she wanted so much more from him, to be in this same exact position only without so many clothes between them.

"Hope…" He dragged his lips beneath the underside of her jaw.

"Hmm?" If she died right now, she would be so happy.

"We should go back to the inn. It is quite cold out here…" But he nipped and nibbled a line of kisses down the side of her throat. "You are shivering."

She met his gaze. The feeling of falling assailed her. Would he catch her? "Perhaps it is not just the cold that is affecting me."

A groan mixed with a growl escaped him, and he again kissed her with such intensity the connection touched her soul. Eventually, he let her up. "Regardless, we need to return. I won't have you catching a head cold merely because we're lingering here."

In a daze, for her head was in the clouds and she floated on the wonderful sensations he'd imparted, Hope nodded. The cold slowly began to seep into her being through the layers of clothing. "The snow is lovely, but this temperature is quite bracing." With a bit of awkwardness, she scrambled off the duke and stood on shaky feet, for her knees had the strength of cooked porridge. *You are quite potent, Your Grace.* She offered a hand to assist him into a standing position. "Regardless, this had been one of the best days of my life."

"That is good to know, but the day is still young." Still grasping her hand, he threaded their fingers together and tugged her through the snow toward the inn once he retrieved his hat. "Who knows what other scandal we can find by the time night falls."

Was there wicked promise in his voice or was her mind playing tricks on her? Perhaps it didn't matter, for the mere suggestion sent heat curling through her insides. "For the moment, we should start with a fire and tea. Once my limbs thaw, we can decide what to do after that." But she smiled. He was proving to be quite a surprising companion.

Too bad they were living on borrowed time at this point.

An hour later, she'd been given a chair by the cheerful crackling fire. Her cloak, gloves, and pelisse had been whisked away by the duke, and when he returned from upstairs, he'd also shed his outerwear, and he'd ordered a pot of tea for them both. He joined her in a comfortable chair of worn leather, and now that she had a cup of tea coursing through her veins to warm her, a certain level of relaxation and drowsiness had come over her.

"Tell me about your family. I would like to know you better," Brook encouraged, and the timbre of his voice was so pleasant that she nodded. The common room wasn't overly full; only half the tables were occupied, and there was a hushed buzz of conversation filling the air. Largely, they were alone and ignored tucked away near the fire.

"Must I?" It would cause her pain to speak of it.

"I would like it above half to learn how you became the woman you are today." Earnestness shone in his eyes, and that slight smile curving his lips enchanted her.

"Very well." As soon as she drained her teacup, he was there to refresh it. Being pampered was rather lovely. "My parents were some of the nicest people I ever knew. With my father being a baronet, I lived a large portion of my life in the country. That was the only life I ever knew."

"He never brought the family to London?"

"Rarely, but then, there was no need." She shrugged. "I was an only child and hadn't come of age."

"Not even when you turned nineteen and finished schooling?"

"We did not, but my mother was making plans for such. A Season is rather expensive what with the clothing, the balls and invitations, renting a house, paying for staff." She fixed her gaze on some of the patrons utilizing the common room, for she didn't wish to spy pity in Brook's eyes. "I didn't have one until after I came out of mourning when I lived with my uncle in London for a time."

"You went there after your parents died?" he asked in a soft voice as he touched a hand to her arm. "I'm sure that was a terrible time in your life."

"It was." When her fingers went lax and her teacup flagged, the duke was there to gently take it from her hand. "Three years ago, a fire started in the kitchens. There was no way to determine the exact cause. If it weren't for one of the footmen who woke me, I wouldn't be here today."

"Were your parents the only ones to perish in that fire?"

"No. Most of the staff did too. The footman who saved me went back in for my parents but never returned. One of the maids also was able to get free." Tears filled her eyes.

"Even still, I was burned in the escape and permanently scarred, as I have told you before." She shrugged and wiped at the moisture on her cheeks. "I have become accustomed to my appearance, but it is something that will always ensure I am alone."

"I rather think that won't always be true." He took her hand and squeezed her fingers.

"You are too kind." Hope forced a hard swallow to encourage moisture into her tight throat. "That is why this time with you has been so unique and special," she added in a whisper while meeting his gaze. "Thank you."

"It has been my pleasure. I am sorry for the loss of your family as well as your family home. No one should have to experience something like that." Warmth reflected in his eyes, and once more she was in danger of falling into those blue pools. "Would you like more tea?"

"Yes, please." What a darling man he was, so patient and sympathetic as he waited on her hand and foot. When he gave her the teacup with a grin, flutters danced through her belly. Heightened awareness rippled over her skin and tingled down her spine. "Thank you."

He nodded and then held up a tiny seed cake. "Hungry?"

Yes, but not for food. Aloud, she said, "I hadn't anticipated how much of an appetite I've worked up by playing in the snow." As he brought the cake to her lips, she bit into the sweet and took half. Seconds later, he popped the rest into his own mouth, and they again shared a smile.

"If you don't mind me saying so, seeing such devotion between the two of you warms my heart," the magistrate said as he drifted close to their location.

Hope glanced up at him and blinked, for she'd completely forgotten there were other people in the vicinity. The portly gentleman beamed at her while tugging on the hem of his tweed waistcoat. His thinning brown-gray hair only added to the picture of bucolic living. "I beg your pardon?" She quickly took refuge in her tea to cover the confusion and heat suddenly in her cheeks.

"It is quite obvious you are one of those couples who share the joy of simply being together. All the best marriages have that in them."

Brook chuckled. "I don't know about that, but Mrs. Gerard and I are content."

"Oh, come now. It is more than that. Even a blind man can see the same." The magistrate beamed, and he had the look of Father Christmas. "I was the same way with my wife, God rest her soul. I loved her to distraction."

"I'm sorry to hear you've lost her," Hope murmured and gave him a sympathetic smile. "It seems everyone has someone they've lost, and the missing is more acute during this time of the year."

"Indeed, Mrs. Gerard." The magistrate nodded. "I miss my Sarah every day, but I am heartened when I look about and see her beauty and hear her laughter in many things around me." He winked. "That is how I know she is still with me, always urging me onward, supporting me until we can meet again."

"Oh, that is so sweet and romantic," Hope breathed with a glance to Brook.

He nodded. "I quite agree. Though I miss my, er, ah, certain other people in my life who have gone before, they are always there in our hearts, perhaps guiding us onto a different path we might not have thought to tread before," he finished with a frown and a look of confusion.

"I apologize for interrupting your time." As a string of giggling reached their location, he gestured toward a young couple in the opposite corner. "Do you see them? They have that special something as well." His eyes twinkled as he landed his attention back onto her and Brook. "It is the same as what you two share. Love is the one thing we all search for and when we find it, we cling to that magic with all our strength. Enjoy it while you can."

"Thank you." Hope smiled. "I appreciate your words of insight. Perhaps we can talk to you later this evening."

"Of course, Mrs. Gerard. The snow has given me an unprecedented opportunity to know my fellow travelers better, and perhaps we all need that during this time of year."

Once he left them to speak with the young couple, she glanced at the duke. "I suppose our play acting has convinced everyone here."

"We are ready to tread the boards on Drury Lane indeed." When he caught her gaze, the two of them shared a laugh. "Truth to tell, though, this has been the best of all distractions. I'd suffered from melancholy before coming here, but thanks to you, I feel as if I am ready to take on the world, to perhaps try my hand at living again." That warmth in his eyes glowed stronger. "I cannot fathom being stranded with anyone else quite as lovely."

"I am glad." Unexpectedly, a piece of her heart went into his keeping. This would be a Christmas gift to herself, and she would hug it to her heart for the remainder of her days to keep her company once she'd consigned herself to being a companion and meeting her lonely life.

Without him. She covered the urge to cry by taking a sip of tea. *What a ninny I've become.* For the remainder of their time together, she would need to make a concentrated effort to keep her attachment to him in check. Otherwise, their imminent parting would tear her apart.

Chapter Eleven

December 23, 1810
Evening

Brook had never laughed as much as he
had today. It had started with his foray into the
out-of-doors to trek in the snow then continued
through the afternoon when he'd lingered in the
common room to play cards with some of the
other men while Hope had gone to their room
for a nap, but when she'd returned, she'd
donned a pretty, simple gown of a raspberry
taffeta that temporarily stole his ability to
breathe. Now that dinner had been completed,
he and his pretend wife had come into the
common room to talk and joke with some of
their fellow travelers. They had taken quite a bit
of teasing about being a newly married couple
who couldn't be without each other for a long
period of time.

He hadn't minded, especially when the
good-natured jokes had brought a blush to her
cheeks or a sparkle to her eyes. God, she was

beautiful, and so gracious. While he talked with the magistrate and vicar as well as the innkeeper, she had befriended the young couple, who were around her own age. She also spoke to the German princess and her attendant who had passed into the room from their private dinner. No matter what he was doing, he followed her movements with his gaze, much to the amusement of his companions.

There was a festive current running through the patrons as well as the staff, for it was the Christmastide season, and from the snatches of rumors he'd heard, there would be a party of men sent out tomorrow on the hunt for evergreen boughs as well as holly to decorate the common room. Indeed, the roads were still largely impassable, but if the temperatures kept warming and if rain swept in, the bulk of the snow would recede, and travel could resume.

Brook shoved that terribly sad thought from his mind, for he wasn't quite ready to part from this pretend life he'd invented for himself. "A round of beer for everyone tonight on me!" he said on an impromptu yell. Calls and whoops echoed about the room. "It is Christmastide, my friends, and my wife is exceedingly lovely tonight. That alone is reason to celebrate." When a blush filled her cheeks, he grinned.

"Do stop, Brook," she whispered and pressed a hand to her face. "What has gotten into you?"

What indeed? He was hardly drunk, but this interlude—this woman—had entered his blood and had become an integral part of him. In a myriad of tiny ways, she was changing him, guiding him whether she was aware of it or not, and he didn't mind.

One of the grooms came into the room just as he'd made his announcement. "There will be a good fog in the morning, I'm thinking, for it's warming slightly now. Roads should be reachable in three days or so."

Thank the lord. "Here's to spending Christmas at The Brown Hare Inn!" He hefted his tankard and grinned when the bulk of the room put forth huzzahs.

Hope merely shook her head, but amusement sparkled in her eyes, and he reveled in that. Never had he enjoyed his time more since Deborah had passed from this world.

As the evening drew onward, Brook indulged in a few brandies while Hope partook in a glass of madeira. High spirits abounded throughout the room, but eventually, he wanted her to himself, for he'd come to expect that once night fell outside the inn.

He stood and offered his hand. "Perhaps we should retire, Mrs. Gerard. It has been a long day, don't you think?"

"Perhaps." But she slipped her hand into his palm and smiled when he tugged her into a standing position.

The magistrate chuckled. "Everyone bid the newlyweds goodnight, while the rest of us marinate in our jealousy."

"He is rather over the top," Brook whispered to her as they made their way to the staircase to snickers and much teasing. Yet it was lovely to think that he belonged in a relationship again, even if it was merely a bit of fiction.

What would he do when the façade faded, and they were forced to part ways?

That is a worry for another day.

Once they reached their shared room and he lit one of the candles, and she regarded him with an inscrutable expression, his chest tightened. "Why are you looking at me like that?"

It took next to no time to divest himself of his jacket, cuffs, collar, and cravat. The garments he tossed toward the foot of the bed, not really caring if they made it or not. "How am I looking at you?" His spirits were still buoyed by the events of the day and perhaps fueled by the brandy on top of the beer, but as he removed his waistcoat and tossed it to the floor, he prowled toward her while she retreated to the window.

"Like you wish to scoop me up and devour me… or perhaps abscond with me." Her eyes were round, filled with both confusion and longing as she gazed at him. "I don't know how to interpret that."

"Mmm." The fact she was so perceptive enhanced the desire he'd labored under since that kiss in the snow this morning. "Perhaps I wish to extend what you started out in the woods." When she moistened her lips, he barely stifled a groan. "Or perhaps I should treat you to the same ecstasy you gave me last night." Never had he anticipated a proposal more, for the past two evenings had been spent in some sort of carnal pursuit.

A tiny gasp escaped her, and the window at her back prevented further flight. "Do you think that is a good idea? We are already flirting with going beyond scandal as it is." Those expressive eyes darkened, so she wasn't as uninterested as she wished for him to think.

Surely, I am slowly descending into madness.

"It's not as if anything we do now will erase that." Brook didn't care. His wife was gone; she wasn't coming back. And though his head realized that nothing could come from a dalliance with Hope, his heart—as well as his shaft—argued that the connection they shared deserved at least some initial investigation. "Where you are concerned, pleasure is always a good idea." She was so dewy eyed and pretty in that gown, and damn if he didn't want her, craved that closeness and intimacy they'd enjoyed the night before.

For a long time afterward, he was never certain which of them moved first, but then she was in his arms, and he kissed her as if he hadn't seen a woman for a decade. Oh, she was so soft and warm, and the faint taste of the wine she'd had earlier came away on her lips made the embrace that much sweeter.

The way she twined her hands about his neck, the delicate press of her body against his, the faint scent of her violet perfume, the softness of her lips on his as she kissed him back all worked to remove him from the remainder of his sanity and commonsense. Over and over, he drank from her like a man possessed, and when that wasn't enough, Brook held her head between his hands to better deepen the kiss as he chased her tongue with his, and when he needed more, he plucked the pins from her hair. They pinged slightly as they fell to the floor, but once her brown tresses tumbled about her back and shoulders, he fisted his hands into the thick mass and kissed her anew.

It was all too easy to tug the gown from her frame. She hadn't worn stays, no doubt due to the fact she couldn't operate that garment by herself, but he didn't mind. It only meant one less obstacle keeping him from seeing her body.

Damn, but he'd forgotten how lovely it was to undress a woman. It seemed ages since he'd last done that, for Deborah had been increasing before she'd died, and too many times she wasn't of a mind to be intimate, but it felt all too right with Hope. And she wasn't a passive participant in the embrace. While he manipulated the ties of her petticoat, she pressed her lips to the underside of his jaw, the side of his neck, or shoved her hands beneath his fine lawn shirt once she'd tugged it from his breeches. The heat of her spurred him onward, and when she was clad in her shift, he paused. Should he undress her fully or leave her the modesty of keeping the garment on?

"Brook?" Hope brushed a fingertip over one of his nipples, and electric sensation rushed through him, making him hiss with acute need. "Why do you hesitate?" The same desire bedeviling him clouded her eyes as she peered up at him. Was she even aware of that?

In the guttering candlelight, the burn scars on the inside of her right arm were all too noticeable. "I don't wish to expose your scars if they are something that brings you discomfort." Ardor aside, if she wasn't comfortable, they would go no further.

"Oh." Her fingers stilled on his skin, and when she pulled away from him, he immediately missed her warmth. "You are far too considerate, but perhaps it is time to face my fears." As he watched, she stepped out of the petticoat and then slowly, ever so slowly, she pulled the thin shift from her person. Briefly, it dangled from a finger before slipping to the floor unheeded. Then she stood, more or less nude, before him. The stockings and slippers only added to the eroticism of the action. Tears gathered in her eyes. "I apologize if the scars are too ugly or if they disgust you."

"Ah, Hope." The trust she extended to him left him humbled and honored. "You are beautiful." Twisted, mottled pink skin decorated the right side of her body, but those patches didn't distract from the woman she was nor her charms. He pushed the waterfall of her hair over a shoulder to better admire her form. "Never forget that."

"Such gammon." The whispered protest sounded overly loud in the silence of the room. "I am well aware of what I look like now." When she attempted to turn, to angle her body away from his regard, he slipped a hand about her waist and pulled her closer.

"You are incredibly brave. Much braver than I could ever hope to be." While he'd hidden from life due to being lost in grief, she could never hide from what had happened to her. Not knowing what else to do, Brook gently claimed her lips, kissed away the salty trace of the tears on her cheeks, and as he sought to bring her comfort, his heart shivered to life, came away from the walls he'd kept around that organ. "The scars are proof that you survived, and the world is so much better for the simple fact you are in it."

"I wish more men thought as you do." She plucked at his shirt. "Take this off. I want to explore you."

"Not before I do the same to you." He removed the garment with alacrity and tossed it away. "Tonight, is for your pleasure, not mine."

"But—"

"No," he interrupted and then escorted her to the side of the bed. "You gave me that last night. Now it's your turn." Brook kissed her while making her sit. "I shall be with you in a moment." His chest tightened when she offered a sound of protest, and quickly he toed off his boots, kicking them away. Then he kneeled before her. "I don't take lightly the gift you've given me by letting me see you at your most vulnerable."

"I know you would never hurt me." She braced herself with her palms on the mattress behind her, which put her perfect smallish breasts on display, the pink tips pebbled and all too tempting.

"Never." With slow movements so she wouldn't startle, he removed her slippers and then he untied the ribboned garters. In some amusement, he noted his shaking hands, for it had been a long time indeed since he'd pleasured a woman, but Hope watched him with wide eyes and slightly parted lips, and the picture she made further hardened his length. As best he could, Brook ignored his own need and rolled the stocking down on first one leg. Then he did the same to the other. Oh, she had beautiful limbs, and it mattered not the burn scars marred one of them. "If you feel I've gone too far, tell me nay and I will immediately stop."

She nodded, and when he cupped her breasts, pressed himself closer between her naturally splayed legs, a shuddering breath escaped her. "Brook, I... ooh..."

"Good?" When she nodded, he brushed the pads of his thumbs over her nipples and grinned when a shiver racked her shoulders. "I shall take that for a yes." He dipped his head, licked one of those lovely buds, and then took it into his mouth.

A long moan issued from her and one of her hands fisted in the bedclothes.

It was all the permission he required, and for the next few moments, Brook explored her body with his fingers, his tongue, and his lips. By the time he tugged her to the edge of the bed and encouraged her to recline backward, he was so hard he didn't know if he'd be able to bring her to release without spending in his breeches. Yet, this night was for her alone. Putting all thought to his own comfort to the back of his mind, Brook caressed the inside of her thighs, urged them as far apart as they could comfortably go. "Ready?"

Those creamy thighs quivered. Anticipation and worry mixed in her gorgeous eyes. "Surely you cannot mean to…"

"Oh, but I do, and I will, love." He winked. "It is my fondest hope you will thoroughly enjoy this exercise."

"I… No one has ever done… Oh!" Her squeal of surprise when he licked that warm flesh at her center tugged a snort from him.

"There is no time like the present to explore… everything." The act of pleasuring a woman orally was something he secretly enjoyed, but his wife hadn't let him do it often. From all accounts, Hope liked this type of play, for she'd rested a hand at the back of his head and urged him closer.

As he spread her open with one hand, he continued to caress the inside of her thighs with the other. Easily he found the pearl at her center, teased it with his tongue, and she shook with the beginnings of sensation. Soon, he settled on a rhythm he liked, and he repeated the cycle of teasing, suckling, and licking. The half-stifled sounds Hope made would drive him mad, and each one was more frantic than the last. Tiny pinpricks of pain kept him on the edge as she pulled his hair and squirmed in his hold only enhanced his own desire, and when she bucked her hips against his mouth, he grinned, hummed at her flesh for she was close.

"Brook, I need..." Her body shook and she tossed her head. "...something."

Poor thing. She truly had never been brought to release. Once more, he silently cursed her former fiancé for not properly taking care of her, for not cherishing her, to not loving her as she deserved to be loved.

"Don't fight it, but let the wave take you." Again, he applied himself with renewed effort at that slippery button and dared to penetrate her passage with first one finger and then another. Her gasp of surprise echoed on the air. Dear God, she was so tight and definitely still an innocent. He'd need to be careful, but oh how he wished he could feel that honeyed heat snug around his member.

Then a strangled sort of scream ripped from her throat the second he suckled hard at the nubbin, and he grinned as Hope fell into her first foray of carnal bliss. Gentle contractions tremored around his fingers, and his shaft pulsed in response. Damn, he'd never been so hard, but the discomfort was forgotten as he watched the expressions flit over her face— wonder, pleasure, amazement, exhaustion. Though he'd thought her beautiful before; now she was ethereal, angelic, transcendent in that bliss when her back arched and she squirmed while he continued to tease that tiny bundle of nerves.

"Brook!" Near hysterical, Hope collapsed fully onto her back. One hand drifted to a breast to pluck at a pink nipple, and he almost shot his wad right there. "That was... I feel so... No one told me..."

He couldn't help but grin. No matter where their paths led or what the future held, she would always remember this moment and him, for he had been the first man to make her come by oral stimulation, and what was more, he wasn't quite finished with her yet.

"That was merely one tiny part of intimacy," he whispered as he climbed onto the bed to join her. In her lethargy, she glanced at him, and there was such heated invitation in those eyes, he had no recourse except to bite the inside of his cheek and ignore the throbbing need in his highly aroused shaft.

"Good heavens. There is more?" She crawled up and then collapsed against the pillows.

"So much more." Needing the distraction, Brook covered her body with his. He kissed her as if there was nothing else to do in this life and alternately as if he were running out of time. Her hands were everywhere on him, caressing, touching, exploring, and he did the same to her. Though it would take years to learn the secrets of her body, he set out to at least try, and whenever he touched or nibbled at a part of her that made her cry out in pleasure, he was eager to find the next.

Wanting to make her spend once more, he slipped a hand between her thighs. The damp curls shrouding her sex sent a shiver of pure desire down his spine, for if he were to spear into her right now, would she be slick and welcoming? He strummed his fingers over her swollen button while he teased a breast with his tongue and lips.

She shattered more quickly this time, and more spectacularly. As her scream erupted, he slammed his mouth onto hers in the attempt to take the sound into himself. The last thing he wanted was anyone in the surrounding rooms to get their rocks off knowing Hope was being thoroughly pleasured. Those sounds were his alone, and he was selfish enough to try and keep them hidden.

There was no doubt that she was completely lost on waves of pleasure, but so was he, only on something entirely different. What the devil was he going to do, for he recognized the initial feelings. This time at the Brown Hare Inn wasn't reality and neither could it continue on past being stranded. He had his life and she had hers; they were from two different worlds, and besides, he was still very much in love with his wife, wasn't he?

Bloody hell, but that line was blurred.

When her body came down from the heights of bliss and her trembles receded, Brook rolled onto his back, as exhausted as if he'd coupled with her. She blew out a breath, looked at him with such hunger in her eyes that he had to bear down in order to stave off spending. "Finish me, Your Grace. I want all of you."

Those words, he feared, were the beginning of his undoing, but he shook his head. As much as it pained him, as much as it went against everything he wanted in this moment, he had to deny her. "I cannot."

"Why? Clearly, you are in need." When she glanced her fingers over his rampant length behind his frontfalls, he shuddered and prayed he wouldn't explode.

"This is true, but you are an innocent, and you should remain as such for when you find a decent man… the man you will eventually marry."

"You and I both know that will never happen." Tears welled in her eyes. She removed her touch from his person. "Not while my fate lies in becoming a lady's companion."

It didn't matter that she was right. In this he would remain firm. "That gift, your innocence, belongs to the man you will fall in love with." He swallowed hard to encourage moisture into his suddenly tight throat. "You deserve that, Hope. You deserve to be in love with the man you'll lie with."

And he'd nearly taken that from her through lust alone.

I must do better, for I respect her too much for a casual tryst.

Yet the sensation of falling assailed him, the feeling of belonging he couldn't shake. He'd had that with Deborah and had never experienced it since.

Except now.

"You are quite mean, do you know that?" Her pout was adorable; the flush of arousal on her chest and cheeks lovely.

"You will thank me later." Unable to remain parted from her, he gathered her into his arms with her backside flush to his front. The sensations that crashed through him when his erection brushed her bottom had the power to break him, but he ignored them as best he could. "Once emotions are involved, the act means so much more. I want that for you."

"What if I want something else entirely?" she asked in a barely audible voice.

"I honestly don't know." As he willed his body's reaction to settle, he held her close, nuzzled the crook of her shoulder, and he sighed. Moonlight drifted in through the window to frost everything with a sheen of silver. For the first time since he'd been forced into mourning, he was... content. Shock tightened his chest.

Was that a disservice to Deborah's memory, or was it a sign he was ready to live — and love — again? There were no easy answers.

Eventually, he fell into a light doze to the scent of violets and the undeniable warmth of Hope's body next to his.

Chapter Twelve

December 24, 1810
Christmas Eve afternoon

Hope had decided to take tea in her bedchamber, for the duke was apparently having a wonderful time talking politics and various aspects of the war with a handful of the men downstairs. She didn't mind, for she wanted some time to herself, and she suspected that socializing would be good for him as well.

Between sips of tea, she tidied the room and straightened the bedclothes. That morning, she and Brook had stayed abed rather late, which meant they'd missed breakfast. After the paces he'd put her through the night before, she'd been claimed by exhaustion. By the time she'd woken, he'd already left the room, but there was a plate containing two pieces of toast as well as a small bowl of porridge waiting for her at the bedside with a hastily scribbled note from her pretend husband.

It had been a lovely gesture, and she continued to luxuriate in the feeling of letting a man look after her well-being. Once she'd finally risen and eaten the small offering, she'd rung and asked the maid who answered the bell for a pitcher of warm water. The boon was unexpected, and she used it to clean and refresh her body the best she could without the use of a bathtub.

Through it all, memories from what had happened the night before with the duke flitted through her mind. Never in her life did she think a woman could know such pleasure as what he'd given her; it had certainly been an eye-opening experience, and though she'd wanted to scream with frustration when he wouldn't couple with her, his explanation as to why had both flattered and saddened her.

Once she was delivered to his aunt in Yorkshire, would she ever have the opportunity to see him again? Beyond that, would she have a chance to meet anyone in society that might bring a courtship into her life?

There was no way to know and worrying about it only stole the joy from what she had now. Hope took another sip of tea then scribbled a few lines into her notebook. Something about the duke inspired her to writing, and it was only natural the hero in her story had taken on characteristics of her pretend husband. Tomorrow was Christmas, and since she was still stranded at the inn with everyone else, she would make the best of the situation that she could.

As she hummed a favorite carol, Hope went to her trunk. From the bottom she pulled a carefully folded red silk ballgown. Though it was nearly three years old, the style was still popular. She stood, shook out the garment and then held it up against herself. Since tonight would start the holiday festivities, she would wear it down to dinner regardless of if it was too fancy for such an occasion. The color was cheerful and lifted her spirits, and she adored how the silk felt against her skin. It was the finest dress she owned. Would the duke think her as pretty as other women of his acquaintance?

There were rumors the common room would be decorated tonight with fir boughs and holly if the hunting party was successful today, and one of the maids had let slip there would be spiced rum punch and a few special sweets after dinner tonight, perhaps even dancing if they could find someone to play music.

If only for one night, Hope would pretend she were Brook's duchess, would bask in the happiness she'd found in pretending to be married to him for the past handful of days. Already, this trip had been the best of her life, and she intended to hoard each moment to her heart as a miser hoarded coins.

After draping the gown over the bed, she moved to the window with a glance of longing at the notebook sitting on the bed. Sunlight flooded the outside world, making the snow sparkle, but there was no doubt some of the fluffy whiteness that clung to tree branches and shrubbery was already melting. All too soon, the lives of everyone beneath this roof would return to normal, and this small interruption would soon be forgotten by most people.

But how could she ever forget the time spent with the duke? He had already changed her life, made her think differently about herself and about how she should be treated. Those words and actions would carry her far, for no longer would she let anyone overlook her merely because of her scars.

When the door to the room snicked open, she whirled about. "Brook?" A frown tugged the corners of her mouth downward. "What are you doing here?" And why the devil did he have a sprig of holly clutched in one hand?

"Can not a man wish to spend time with his wife?"

Her heart trembled, for their marriage was pretend, and that was the only way it could be. "Do stop. You know as well as I we are not wed."

For a few seconds, confusion reflected in his eyes, gone at his next blink. "As long as we are at The Brown Hare, you *are* my wife, and I am your husband." Oh, those words were both a balm and a knife to the heart! "Some of the men assembled a party to fetch fir boughs and such while the others went off to parts unknown. I was seized by the urge to talk with you. In all seriousness, you have been as constant as a best friend to me since we arrived here, and I've rather grown used to it." Somberness fell over him. "You are not afraid of my title, and when I'm with you, I feel as if I have the freedom to be myself."

Her heart skipped a beat. "Though you are a duke, you are also a man with strengths and weakness, the same as all of us, and knowing you are not invincible makes you all the more attractive." For long moments they stared at each other while tension filled the air. "Truth be told, I have enjoyed our time together. You are a good listener, and you certainly are supportive." Never would she forget how safe and secure she'd felt while in his arms.

"Ha." He snorted. "I hope I give decent advice, but I'm afraid I'm rubbish at it."

"Don't minimize the wonderful man you are. There is no shame in anything that has come to pass while we've been here." And whether he was aware of it or not, he'd shown the beginning signs of growth. If she had a small part in helping him move through his grief, she would count herself happy.

Sandra Sookoo

"Perhaps." As he came forward, his gaze fell upon the gown. "Do you plan to wear that tonight?"

"Yes." She quickly moved to the bed, took up the gown, and held it up to herself. "Do you think it too much?"

"I think it will be just the thing to lift everyone's spirits. The cut and color are stunning."

"The gown was left over from my singular Season. Do you think it too outdated?" Suddenly, she very much wished to be at her best tonight as a reflection of him—her pretend husband.

"That style is timeless." Admiration and raw need lined his face. "And quite frankly, I cannot wait to see you in it." When he grinned, butterflies danced a ballet in her lower belly. "I brought this sprig of holly up figuring you could put it into your hair tonight, but now it will be a lovely accompaniment to that gown."

"You are a sweet man, Your Grace." She used the formal title to remind herself this wasn't a romance playing out like one of the fairy stories she adored reading. Carefully laying the gown back upon the bed, she sighed as he rested the holly on top of it. "Should there be dancing tonight, I wonder if you will stand up in a set with me."

"Of course, and I'll dare any other man to cheat me out of that prize." There was a certain

175

note of possession in his voice that sent a thrill sailing down her spine.

"Ah, you are good for a woman's ego. No wonder your wife loved you to distraction. You make it so easy." A gasp escaped her as shock went through his eyes. "Oh, I apologize for speaking about a subject that brings you pain." Goodness, would he catch that tiny slip of the tongue? Her feelings toward him were confusing, and if she wasn't careful, she'd lose her heart completely to him.

Like a ninny.

After knowing him only a handful of days.

"No, it is quite all right. I suppose you have the right of it." He rubbed a hand along the side of his face. "Deborah always said I was too charming when I had the right motivation."

She moved to the window and peered outside. It was safer than looking him in the eye or letting him see the emotions in hers, for she'd never learned how to mask her feelings. "I have no doubts she knew you loved her, even to the last." The flit of a bird's wings into the trees captured her attention. So much freedom a bird had! What must it feel like to fly. Then a tiny smile curved her lips. Perhaps it felt like what Brook had given her when she'd tumbled into bliss last night.

"I hope so." A choking sort of sob escaped into the room, and when she glanced into the glass just right, she could see his reflection. He'd put his thumb and forefinger to his eyes. Was he crying? "Did you know she was unconscious a few minutes before she expired?"

"I didn't realize that." And he'd not told her when he'd talked a couple days ago about her passing. "Perhaps that spared her much pain as well as the knowledge her babe had died." Though, to be fair, if there truly was a world beyond this one, Deborah had probably already been reunited with the child.

"There wasn't an opportunity to tell her goodbye or even that I loved her," he admitted in a barely audible whisper.

The raw emotion in those words pulled at her chest. Hope turned about. "Is that why you have kept yourself aloof from everyone and not rejoined society? You fear you failed your wife at the last?"

"I don't know." He seemed so dejected and almost lost that compassion propelled her feet into motion.

"From everything you have shared with me, the two of you were well matched. A bond such as yours would have been evident even to the last." She laid a hand on his arm. The muscles tensed beneath her fingertips. "Please don't torture yourself further, Brook. I am quite certain Deborah wouldn't have wanted that."

"Perhaps you are right." His eyes were haunted as he met her gaze. "It's what troubles me the most. She just… left, and I had no say in the matter."

Tears stung the backs of her eyelids. "I haven't thought about death in that way before, but it makes sense." Her chin quivered. "The night of the fire, I wasn't given the chance to say goodbye to my parents either." Would it have made a difference? They would have perished anyway. Would saying additional words have given her more peace than she had now? There was no way to know. "They were gone and then I was alone."

"Yes, exactly." His eyes were red-rimmed. "It keeps me awake at night."

"You poor thing." On impulse, Hope stood on her toes, wrapped her arms about him, and held him close. To her astonishment, he trembled and held her tightly back. For long moments, they simply stood there without words, being with each other in mutual grief. "Perhaps the nights when you cannot sleep, you should think of something that brings you hope."

He chuckled. "I already have Hope. At least for the moment."

Truly, he was a dear. "I shall never tire of your jokes regarding my name." Worry knotted in her belly. *What will I do without him?*

"Good." But he didn't release her. Instead, he took a few steps to the side and then tumbled them both onto the bed. Her notebook fell off and landed with a thud on the hardwood.

With a squeak of surprise, she tried to squirm away, but he caught her into his arms again and snuggled into her. "What are you doing?" Would he treat her to more of the naughty things he'd done last night? Her breathing quickened merely from thinking of it.

"Hush now. I merely wished to lie here and continue our talk. At least until it's time to dress for dinner."

Easily enough, she settled into his arms. She wriggled her bottom, and part of her rejoiced when the brush of his erection made itself known. "This time of year makes me maudlin, I'm afraid. There is much about my parents that I miss; much about the manor I miss, which is silly, for it was just a pile of bricks, really."

"But it was your home for the whole of your life. There is no shame in that, Hope." The solid feel of his arms coupled with the baritone tenor of his voice all washed over her and spun a cocoon of acceptance around her. Tears filled her eyes for a different reason entirely than grief. "What made the house special to you?"

"Oh, so many things. I liked the ivy that grew up one side of the brickwork." So many times as a child she pretended she resided in a fairy's cottage in the middle of the forest. "Then there were two oak trees that had grown up twisted near the rear of the manor. I liked to think they were once spritely lovers but were cursed by a god, forever locked in an embrace."

"I can imagine you were a handful for your parents with an imagination like that."

"Now you know why I enjoy writing stories." She closed her eyes. The man smelled too good. He was temptation personified, but she shoved that thought away. "At Christmastide, my mother made certain each room on the lower level of the house had some sort of decoration. Our house always smelled like evergreens and citrus, and sometimes spices if we could afford them."

"That sounds lovely."

"It was. At dinner on Christmas, we would exchange small gifts. Simple things that meant something special."

"We didn't do much of that, but I think perhaps it was something that is becoming more and more the fashion now." He pressed his lips to her temple. "My family threw lavish balls and even house parties to celebrate the holiday. There were rich foods and luxurious clothing, dancing by music on the pianoforte, and sometimes there were parlor games and pantomimes."

It was another reminder their worlds were vastly different. "Sometimes, we would attend church services at midnight and then walk home in the chilly night. Those were favorite times too, for if the skies were clear, there were thousands of twinkling stars. It used to remind me we were never alone."

Another long stretch of time went by marked by silence. Laughter and muted talking echoed in the corridor. No doubt some of the inn's patrons coming up to dress for dinner. Hope had nearly drifted off to sleep when the rumble of Brook's voice brought her awake.

"It is my sincere hope you will one day find your work published. I shall be one of the first people to buy a copy of your books, merely for the pleasure of saying I knew you before you became the people's darling."

Yes, he was much too charming. Drat his eyes. "If you come out to Yorkshire, I shall sign the books for you. Otherwise, perhaps the income from selling such things will be modest enough that I can rent a small cottage nearer to London…" Her voice broke, for the days were growing perilously short. Soon enough she would leave this man's company, and she doubted she would see him again. "Promise me you will let me say goodbye, though before you leave me alone with your aunt."

"Of course I will." The duke held her a tiny bit tighter. "Rest before dinner. I am going to ring for some hot water so I might bathe as best I can with a towel and the basin." He bussed her cheek and then left the bed. "Ah, Hope, you have no idea how much this snowbound reprieve has meant." The words were so low she had to strain to hear them.

Had he meant to utter them aloud? But she allowed a secret smile, secure in the knowledge he couldn't see her since her back was to him and the washstand. She would enjoy the night and damn the worry over her future. Wriggling to the edge of the bed, she retrieved her notebook and pencil. There were thoughts she wished to jot down in her story, for the duke had made an impression on her she wouldn't soon forget.

With a glance out the window at the darkening skies, she looked for the brightest star that wasn't yet visible. Once it was, though, perhaps she would make a wish. For just one night—a special Christmas night—she wanted to know what it felt like to be loved by a man.

Him.

Then she would accept her fate and go to Yorkshire without complaint.

Chapter Thirteen

December 24, 1810
Christmas Eve Evening

Brook groaned as he pushed his plate away. "I must say, I didn't think we would have eaten as well as we did while stranded at a posting inn, but the cook here has shown me how wrong I have been."

Once more he and Hope had enjoyed a dinner in one of the private dining rooms, but the low buzz of conversation and laughter drifted to his ears. Obviously, festivities were beginning in the common room, and oddly enough, he wished to be a part of that.

Beyond that, unbeknownst to his lovely companion, he'd traded two books he'd tucked away in his trunk to the German princess for a set of dainty, lace-edged handkerchiefs he would give to Hope on Christmas to mark the occasion. It was the best he could do in the situation, but he suspected she would be pleased.

And it would gain him a soft smile, perhaps the one she reserved for him. Was she even aware she did that?

"It is good to have preconceptions challenged every once in a while," she said with a grin as she laid her silverware across her empty plate. "The roast beef was excellent, I'll agree."

"Too stuffed for dancing?" Damn, but she was easily the most beautiful woman beneath this roof tonight, he'd wager, and in that cheerful gown of red silk, never would he pass another Christmas without thinking of her and how she looked just now with happiness twinkling in those doe-brown eyes and her kissable lips curved in a mischievous smile. Though she had donned a woolen shawl, not once did she seem self-conscious about the burn scarring on the inside of her right arm. He hoped a tiny piece of that confidence had come from his encouragement and assurances she was beautiful as she was.

"Of course not. It is something I have looked forward to for the past day." One of her finely feathered eyebrows rose in challenge. She'd tucked the spring of holly he'd given her into her upswept hair. It rested just over her left ear, and it completed the most fetching picture he'd ever seen. "Are you?"

"Not by half." Compared to her, the evening attire that was *de rigueur* for men of the *ton* in London at social events seemed slovenly and dull. Hope's red gown and her easy temperament made tonight a special occasion indeed. Slowly, he stood and then offered her a hand. "Shall we adjourn and join our fellow travelers?"

"That would be lovely." The moment she slipped her fingers into his palm, warmth tingled up his arm to his elbow. Once she gained her feet, she smiled up at him. "What would you be doing at home tonight if you weren't stranded here?"

He tucked her hand into the crook of his elbow as he escorted her from the room. "Well, I would no doubt be cooling my heels in my aunt's drawing room." Had it not been for the snowstorm, he wouldn't have come to know Hope on such a personal level. "I would have brought you to Yorkshire as I'd been tasked. We would have gathered in that drawing room where my aunt would have regaled me with a list of complaints about the house and the staff or told me all about her latest ailments or how humanity has failed her yet again." His chest tightened and he drew her to a halt just inside the doorway that led into the common room. "You would have been relegated to the background, deferring to my aunt's whims, only talking when she acknowledged you, and I would have been deprived of knowing the true woman behind the necessity of taking a position."

"It's interesting that since our paths crossed at a different moment, the outcome was much more rewarding than it might have been." Yet the delicate tendons in her throat worked with a hard swallow. "I am glad I was given the opportunity to know you this way instead of what was to be our lot. You are nothing like I assumed."

That didn't stop the panic and feeling of dread from climbing his spine. Sooner or later, he would need to complete his original task of delivering her to his aunt. This deviation at the inn, no matter how lovely and inspiring, wouldn't last. Once the roads cleared, they would no longer have cause to pretend at being married and would need to return to the people they'd always been meant to be.

Without ever meeting in such a close capacity again.

Truly, that was a dismal thought. "This has been... Er, what I mean to say is—"

"Come now, Mr. Gerard. Join us!" The magistrate's hail interrupted what he would have said and scattered his thoughts. The older man gestured for him to enter the common room. "Some of the younger folks have indicated a wish for dancing. Give us a hand in moving the furniture? That is if you can tear yourself away from your wife's side for a few minutes?"

Good natured laughter circled through the assembled company. Many of the occupants of the room were dressed in their best clothes. No doubt everyone wished to make use of the fine garb since they wouldn't reach their Christmastide destinations. It was a comforting sight to see all these people from different walks of life and social structures come together in order to celebrate a common goal.

"I… uh…" In some confusion, he glanced at Hope, who watched him with amusement in her eyes, but in their depths was a trace of sadness. The same thing bedeviled him beneath the façade he wished to show to everyone else. When she nodded, he sighed. "Of course."

"I'm not going anywhere," she said in a low voice. "Go spend the time with your new friends. It's good for you and will assist you in deepening relationships with your tenants and others under your responsibility."

Yes, this world was quite different from the one in which he resided, and he needed that reminder. "Of course." How had she become such a guiding force in a handful of days? It was something he'd missed since the death of his wife, and it was something he was learning about himself; he needed someone to advise and support him, to perhaps show him the best opportunities or choices he should make.

As soon as he joined the magistrate and the vicar, who were moving tables and chairs to one side of the room, the older man teased him.

"I must say, Mr. Gerard, your wife is Christmas personified. You are a lucky man, indeed." The magistrate glanced in Hope's direction and gave her a wave. When she waved back, he grinned. "Her presence here sure brightens up a difficult situation."

"Yes, she certainly does." Brook sent his gaze across the room where Hope had moved to speak with the young widow and her small boy. When she kneeled to talk to the child at his level, his heart squeezed, and unexpectedly a piece flew into her keeping. She wasn't timid or retiring, and it didn't seem that she knew a stranger. Once she'd gained confidence in herself, there wasn't anything she couldn't do. "I am a fortunate man, as you said."

Except, all of this was a ruse, a bit of fiction put forth to circumvent scandal, of which they'd indulged in anyway.

"By the by," the vicar said, and Brook directed his attention to the man who perhaps of an age with him. His black hair gleamed almost blue beneath the candle lights. "What is your livelihood, Mr. Gerard? I don't believe anyone has ever mentioned it."

Hell's bells.

Why hadn't he thought to flesh out the lie more thoroughly? "Er, I am in banking, actually." That sounded like a tidy, respectable way to make a living. "Have always been fond of toting up columns of numbers and do a fair job of accounting." His laugh sounded all too forced to his ears, but his companions didn't appear as if they'd noticed. "Quite dull at times, I know, but it allows me to travel a bit with my wife."

The magistrate nodded. He put several chairs in a row. "Best do it now before you start a family. Once little ones come, it is difficult enough to do anything let alone travel."

Oh, dear God.

In his mind's eye he saw himself walking about Hyde Park near the Serpentine with a toddler sitting on his shoulder while Hope strolled beside him, her belly swollen with child. Such fanciful musings that could never be, of course, yet the image persisted. The boy had brown hair the same as hers, but blue eyes like his, and no matter that Brook was busy with the banal task of rearranging tables and chairs in the common room of an inn, a longing for the life that daydream represented grew in his chest until he fairly gasped from it.

"Uh, I shall bear that in mind," he finally replied to the nods and knowing glances of the other men.

With a laugh, the magistrate clapped a hand to Brook's shoulder. "You needn't look so shocked, friend. We all know that having a family is the next step after marriage."

"Or even sometimes before those vows, in many cases," the vicar interrupted, and the men laughed again. "Why do you think so many nuptial ceremonies are done in haste?" He waggled his eyebrows. "Much of my time is spent wedding couples who have anticipated things, let's say."

"No harm in that either," the magistrate was quick to add. "Love is love, men. And once it comes for us, there is nothing we won't do to keep it, protect it, hold it close." The mustache on his upper lip quivered when he grinned. "Vicar Bowling, you should ask the innkeeper if he'll bring out his flute or fiddle. I'm of a mood to dance with Mr. Gerard's beautiful wife and perhaps remember my own."

"Indeed, Mr. Pierce." The vicar shot off across the clear expanse of floor with a wide grin.

In short order, the matronly housekeeper brought a bowl of rum punch into the room, and once the treat was shared, laughter and conversation flowed more freely. More logs were thrown onto the fire to create a cheerful, snapping blaze, while a few of the men deposited piles of evergreen boughs on the floor. The women present rooted through the inn's cupboards and storerooms until they were able to procure ribbons and various shiny baubles with which to enhance the boughs. A few oranges studded with cloves complimented the sharp scent of the pine. Then the decorations were laid on the hearth and tacked above doorframes or set upon windowsills. A few more candles were added to further enhance the festive atmosphere.

A game of charades was then declared, and over the course of the next hour, Brook surprised himself by pantomiming and acting out various things for participants to guess at. Much laughter was shared, and time and time again he looked for Hope's shining eyes or listened for her delighted laughter when he did something particularly worthwhile or amusing.

When it was her turn, he marveled at her skill, and the vicar seemed taken with her talents as well. After charades, a few rounds of Blindman's Bluff were enjoyed by the party. Brook declined to participate, but when Hope accepted the blindfold and tried to guess the identity of a few participants, he laughed as heartily as the rest.

Finally, a call for dancing was sent up, and the company agreed. Country reels as well as jigs came in rapid fire. Brook was tugged into the fray to partner various women—including the German princess—who laughed and sang along with the best of them. Hope was a popular partner, of course, but she didn't seem to mind, for she was always laughing, and her cheeks were pleasantly pink from the exertion.

Damn, but he was so proud of her! Hope had blossomed since the snowstorm stranded them all at The Brown Hare Inn. As he followed her progress about the floor while she partnered the magistrate in a particularly lively reel, warmth spread through his chest. Throughout the time here, she had treated everyone equally, made them feel as if they were the only ones in the room and she'd come specifically to see them. That alone had his respect, for that was what was needed from a duchess.

He stumbled and missed a step, forced to apologize to a young lady for stepping on her toes, but then immediately he was lost in his own musings once more. *Did* he want Hope for his next duchess? Was that even an option? After Deborah's death, he promised himself he wouldn't search out love again, for it hurt too much when that love ended, yet after meeting Hope and spending time with her—more than he would have courting her properly in London—he'd come to admire and respect the woman she was... the woman she was growing into with each passing day.

But was she cut out to become a duchess? They were from different worlds and classes. Though she'd been gently bred, had she the wherewithal to withstand scrutiny, gossip, and criticism from tattlemongers and rivals?

The answers weren't immediately forthcoming, and only confusion kept him company.

Then the last set was declared a waltz. Immediately, the floor was filled with couples wishing to participate. Though Hope had a dizzying array of offers, Brook took her hand and gently tugged her away from her circle of admirers.

"Sorry, friends, you have all partnered her at least once this evening, but my wife has promised *this* dance to me." He glanced about with a smile of pride, for she *was* his… at least for the next few days.

She uttered a soft snort. "That wasn't well done of you."

"How do you mean?" He guided her to an open spot on the floor.

"Staking a claim like that."

"Well, I *did* want every man here to know you are mine."

There was no other chance for further conversation, for the first notes of the fiddle had begun and he set them off into the dance. The steps when he partnered her were his favorite, for at each turn or twirl, her skirts brushed his legs. He wished it was a Continental style waltz instead of the more popular Vienna for there was better opportunity to hold a partner close, but this was as magical as anything he'd ever encountered.

One of the times when she came back into his arms, he dared to hold her closer than propriety demanded, and as they clasped hands, he peered into her eyes and whispered, "Can you even imagine what I want to do to you when we are alone again?"

Surprise jumped into her eyes, quickly followed by the same need currently burning through his blood. "Then we shouldn't linger long tonight," she said with a wink before the steps of the dance carried her away once more.

A growl jumped into his throat, for suddenly he didn't want another man partnering her, even if it was expected within the set and for a few seconds. The older woman he was with currently snickered.

"It is refreshing to see a man so smitten with his wife these days." She gave him a smile that showed a gap where a tooth used to be. "That's how my man and I acted when we were your ages."

At the last second, Brook nodded. "Did your feelings fade?" While he'd loved Deborah to the depths of his being, those feelings didn't burn white hot or as intently as what he harbored for Hope.

"Perhaps, but life got in the way. Children came. Worries over money happened." She shrugged as she circled him. "When you take your mate for granted, distance creeps in."

"I will remember that. Thank you."

Once more Hope returned to him, and he breathed a silent sigh of relief.

She laughed at him, much like Deborah used to. "Did you think you might have lost me?"

This night—knowing her over the course of their time at the inn—had changed his life. He needed to think, but right now he was enjoying a party for the first time in a very long while... all because of the woman in his arms. "Honestly? Yes." As the waltz drew to a close, he lost another piece of his heart to her. How was that possible? And more to the point, how could he keep this feeling of perfection with him for longer than his tenure at the inn?

Dear Lord, had he taken leave of his senses? Perhaps not. It *was* the season of miracles, after all, yet it didn't excuse the temporary insanity falling over him. He grinned at Hope, took her hand, and led her off to one side of the room while his mind spun with possibilities, none of which were worthy of his position in society.

Could he? *Should* he? The decision required much more contemplation.

At some point during the dancing, she'd managed to lose the sprig of holly. "What now?" Hope accepted another glass of punch from one of the footmen, and as she drank it, jealousy speared through his chest for the glass that touched those perfect pink lips.

Damn but he wanted her despite the promise he'd made to himself last night that he would keep her an innocent.

"Do you wish to remain here for the next couple of hours and usher in the midnight hour with the remainder of the party?" *Please say no!*

"Not particularly." The light in her eyes promised wicked things. Desire slammed down his spine to lodge into his stones. "Haven't we always retired early while we have been here? It wouldn't seem strange to do so tonight." She squeezed his fingers. "After all, we *are* a married couple, and it is expected we would take to our bed before everyone else."

Would that those words were the truth. But he nodded. "I could read to you." For he couldn't very well announce in front of all these people he wanted nothing more than to take her to bed and spend the next few hours lost in the secrets of her body.

"That sounds like a lovely way to pass the time until we sleep." Yet the smile she gave him brimmed with heat and suggestion enough to harden his length. "Do you wish for another drink before we go?"

"Perhaps I should." For courage. He brought her hand to his lips. "I shall meet you upstairs in a twinkling." And perhaps clarity would be granted to help sort the confusion from the purpose in his mind.

For he rather thought he was two sheets to the wind over her as it was.

Chapter Fourteen

❖━━━❖❖❖━━━❖

December 24, 1810
Christmas Eve night

What a lovely night this has been!

The dancing and socializing and merriment were much better than any she'd ever experienced during her one and only Season in London. Everyone had been in high spirits, and everyone had been so wonderful to each other. Rich or poor, working class or royalty, it had mattered not. Christmas Eve was a time to come together and celebrate love and friendship, which they had all done famously.

Hope still could smell the sharp pine boughs and the cloves in the oranges through the air as she gained the privacy of her bedchamber. Perhaps she'd imbibed on too much rum punch, but it felt as if her feet barely touched the floor as she waltzed herself across the hardwood to the window. Oh, she was drunk on the gaiety of the evening, but she thought that perhaps she was merely inebriated on the duke and how she was beginning to feel about him.

Kicking off her slippers, she rested a palm on the window glass and reveled in the coolness of it against her skin.

Or perhaps it was merely the magic of the night and being happy for the first time in what felt like forever. Because she hadn't yet lit a candle, she was able to peer into the dark woods beyond the window. It beckoned with whispers and secrets as a fox darted about the naked trees. A slow smile tugged at the corners of her lips, for she suspected the real reason to explain her uplifted mood, and it was both wonderful and concerning.

Stupidly, and like a feathers-for-brains ninny just out of the schoolroom, she was falling in love with the Duke of Denton. Or perhaps infatuation was a better term. Did she want his body, want to be claimed by him, want the unrelenting desire circling hungrily through her insides to stop by only his hand?

Oh, yes. There was no denying that.

However, there was something more there, something additional that added to her confusion each time she was in his company. He was sweet in the way he looked after her, and kind in how he got on with the other people stuck together under this roof. Over the course of the days she'd been with him, he'd changed his thinking, perhaps, on a variety of subjects, and she hoped he would carry that new knowledge with him into the future.

Beyond that, he had given her back faith in humanity. It only took one person to see the light in another, regardless if that light had been extinguished years before. Brook had done that, had sheltered the flickering flame deep in her heart so it had the strength to nurture itself back to life. He'd allowed her to once more see herself as whole, to look past the scars on her body and her heart, and he'd assured her she wasn't lacking.

To say nothing that she was immediately happier when he was near. She wanted to know everything about him beyond his history of grief. They hadn't discussed too many other personal things that weren't connected to death and mourning, but since those topics had essentially bound them together, perhaps it didn't matter.

Yet knowing what made him excessively angry, discovering what color he favored, finding out what type of work he liked doing in parliament would be a lovely start. Did he long for children? Was traveling something he wished to do? Beyond his aunt in Yorkshire, did he have any other family? Where was his country estate?

For now, none of that was urgent. She had spent many wonderful hours downstairs and had laughed for the first time in far too many months. Not to put too fine a point on it, the whole delay in her trip had given her back the hope she'd lost when her fiancé had written that letter begging off their engagement.

And she would treasure how it felt always.

"Hope?"

Oh, good heavens, he's here! She hadn't heard the door open, so lost in thought was she. Turning about, she rested her hands on the window ledge. "Brook." In his black evening wear and tailcoat, he was easily the most handsome man she'd beheld in the whole of her life. While her fiancé had had rugged good looks, the duke was classically beautiful, like Italian marble statues, related in a roundabout way to royalty yet as approachable as any of those tradesmen and laborers in the common room. "I didn't hear you come in."

"So I observed." He stood on the opposite side of the room with the bed between them, and for the first time there was uncertainty, a vulnerability, in his expression that gave her pause. "If you don't wish to be disturbed, I can go..."

"No!" On this night of all nights, she wanted to be with him. "I was merely woolgathering, thinking about the party. Truly, it was a wonderful evening."

"Agreed." He shifted his weight, clearly ill-at-ease. "You are as lovely in that gown as I thought you would be." Then the duke smiled, and a rush of flutters went through her lower belly. "I was proud to be your escort tonight, glad of the knowledge that every man in attendance thought you were with me."

"Oh, Brook!" Unwilling or unable to be apart from him, Hope skirted about the bed and threw herself into his waiting arms. She hugged him close. "Thank you for making this holiday stuck in an inn so memorable and wonderful. Without your presence, without knowing *you*, it would have been a miserable endeavor." When she peered up into his face, all her doubts and inhibitions fell away. "Never will I forget this week."

"Neither will I."

In that moment, they were perfectly aligned, and she wanted him, as much as he would give, but she needed to be with him, the consequences be damned. Lifting up onto her toes, Hope held his head between her hands and kissed him. In this man, she had found acceptance and belonging, and they were exactly what she needed at this time in her life.

The press of his lips to hers, the sure insistence of his hands on her hips then sliding up her back left her gasping, selfishly wanting more.

So much more.

As tiny fires licked through her veins, she pulled away merely to find his gaze in the darkness. "I need you, Brook. Please let me be your wife tonight in all the ways that matter." It was a bold statement to be sure, but it was how she felt, and she stood by those words.

Those blue eyes deepened into the most perfect sapphire. "Are you certain?" The hand at the small of her back tightened ever so slightly, and already his other hand worked at the buttons on her gown. "Everything will change if we do this, and I did say you should keep your innocence for the man you would marry." The same desire burning her up from within clouded his eyes. "That is your right."

"Oh, indeed it is." Her heart trembled from his consideration. "But I am old enough to know my own mind, Your Grace, and what I do with *my* body is *my* decision." Again, she pressed her lips to his. "I am giving that gift to you. Without coercion, without the expectation of anything from you other than this night."

For long moments he looked at her, held her gaze, then he nodded. "You have no idea how much I want you, Hope."

"Oh, I have a fair idea." One which she would confirm as soon as his breeches came off. "Take me to bed. Show me I am not wrong about you."

"Ah, sweeting. I think our paths were fated to land here."

She squealed when he hefted her into his arms, holding her beneath the thighs, then took a few steps until the wall at her back halted further movement. As her heartbeat beat out a wild rhythm, she clutched at his shoulders, wrapped her legs about his waist, and kissed him again, for there was no reason not to. The taste of brandy lingered on his lips, and it only enhanced her need, for it was strong, and sharp, and very masculine.

The duke apparently wasn't content to let her have all the fun. He swiftly took possession of the embrace, and all too soon his tongue was in her mouth bossing hers, and the kiss took a dive into wicked, heated territory. Friction from the fabric between their bodies rubbed along her sensitive flesh, and she shivered. A barely audible moan left her throat, and Brook chuckled. "I understand all too much."

Before she knew what he was about, he lifted her once more, and when he gently deposited her on the bed, he followed her down. But he wasn't done. Oh, no. He covered her body with his, treated her to long, drugging kisses that left her heated and floating in a cloud of passion with need zipping through her bloodstream.

There was simply nothing better than having the weight of a man on top of her. His sandalwood and citrus scent teased her nose. She shuddered with anticipation as his hands glided over her skin as he slowly, oh so slowly, removed her gown, petticoat, shift, stockings, and slippers.

"Damn, you are beautiful." The appreciative gleam in his eyes as he devoured her naked form with his gaze sent curls of excitement through her belly. "An angel, surely."

"Do stop, Brook." Yet she couldn't recall her grin of pleasure. No more did she try to hide the scarred portions of her body. But she wanted him as nude as she, so they could finally play with conviction. Hope plucked at the buttons on his waistcoat then tugged at his cravat. "Remove them, please."

"So polite when I half expected a tigress."

She giggled. "The night is still young, Your Grace."

"Such a tart mouth on you." He grinned and followed her command with alacrity. Clothing dropped indiscriminately to the bed and the floor. "Perhaps I should employ it on better endeavors than talking."

"I am game if you are." Just thinking about his mouth on various portions of her anatomy caused her to give in to a shiver.

He waited on his knees, merely so she could look her fill at him. Drat his eyes.

"Once upon a time I assumed all dukes were old, stodgy creatures with garlic breath and a stomach pouch." But not Brook. She couldn't take her attention from him, and finally she had a glimpse of him *sans* breeches. His body was lean and muscled like marble statues of Greek gods, but he wasn't the perfection of those men of legend. In fact, he was better, for he was elegant and honed, muscled as a jungle cat.

"Bah." When he brushed his knuckles over one of her aroused nipples, he laughed as she moaned. "Now whose turn is it to have perceptions challenged?"

"Touché." Those broad shoulders alone could bring her to tears, but her mouth watered at the sight of the ridged, chiseled lines of his chest and abdomen. "I would do many things to lick champagne from your naval." There was no shame in the admission, for they were both here for the same reason. The scattering of blond hair on his chest drew her attention, and with a hand she followed a thin ribbon that went down his body. Dear God, the rampant length of him that sprouted from a nest of blond curls had her gasping even though she'd already tasted that part of him.

"I can ring for some, but I don't know if this inn has anything that fancy in their cellars." His grin was genuine as waggled his eyebrows. "Perhaps you would accept brandy?"

"Hardly. I'll merely content myself with devouring you without accompaniment."

"That can easily be arranged." Once more he came over her body, and this time he kissed her as if he had all the time in the world.

Hope didn't mind, for he was darling in his quest to see her relaxed and comfortable. Everywhere he touched brought out exquisite sensations or sent ripples of awareness sailing over her skin. As best she could, she returned the favor, for she couldn't have enough of his body. The duke was strong and hard in all the places a man should be, but soft and luscious in others. His warm skin was a lovely contrast to the coolness of the room, and when she dragged her lips along the underside of his jaw, the trace of his stubble ignited her need.

"This is better than I could have dreamed," she managed to gasp out before a moan stole further words.

"On this I agree with you." Then he proceeded to kiss and caress every inch of her body. Nowhere was hidden from his notice, not even the burn scars. He explored each one with the same attention he gave the rest of her, and that unwavering devotion brought tears to her eyes. Where her fiancé had used those scars as the reason he couldn't be with her, Brook included them in his love making, and it made all the difference. With each touch, lick, and nibble, she was lifted higher and higher toward that edge of bliss. Brook's hot mouth on her breasts, his tongue teasing her sensitized nipples, his talented fingers between her thighs left her moaning and wriggling with excitement. Her body hummed in heightened need. Each time she reached to fondle his member, he batted her hand away.

"Not yet."

She contented herself by caressing his chest, his shoulders, his back, but her concentration fractured for he was relentless in bringing her pleasure. Slowly, her mind began to shatter. "I cannot survive much more of your torture."

"That is too bad, for I am not nearly done." The warmth of his breath skated over her skin as he kissed a blazing path between her breasts while he kneaded those quivering mounds. Down, down, down he went along her torso, over her stomach, past her mons, kissing and licking and nibbling as was his wont. When he put his mouth over the place, the center of her heat where his fingers had just teased, Hope wasn't prepared. She shook into a million pieces of light. A moan mixed with a slight cry left her throat as she arched her back.

"Merciful heavens, Brook!"

"Hang onto something, love. We are not finished." He ignored her cries and clutching fingers in favor of drawing out her pleasure with tongue and teeth while he worked at teasing the swollen button at her center. When she tugged on his hair as contractions rocked her core, he lifted his head. His chuckle further heightened her need. "Did you need something else?"

"Oh, you…" She panted but urged his head back to where she wanted him. "There will be paybacks."

"I don't doubt it. You are quite determined, but in this I have the upper hand." With a gleam in his eyes that promised wicked things, Brook resumed his work. His fingers dug into her hips, branding her, holding her steady, and on one particularly enthusiastic series of teasing with his tongue, release caught her up in an unexpected vortex.

"Ah!" She tumbled into the void of white light dappled with rainbows as pleasure washed over her body. How he'd managed to toss her over into bliss so quickly, she had no idea.

"Did you wish to say something?" The question rumbled in her chest as he came back up her body.

"You are horrible, do you know that?" This time she didn't take no for an answer as she slid a hand between their bodies. As she wrapped her fingers around his straining shaft, a moan escaped him. "What's good for the goose and all that, Your Grace." Then she nipped the underside of his jaw while slowly pumping her curled fingers up and down his length.

"Mmm. A worthy opponent." When he kissed her again, all thought flew out of her mind. She left off with her torture, and as he spread her thighs wider, he fit the wide head of his member to her opening. "Do you want me, Hope?"

"Do you truly need to ask?" She found his gaze in the darkness. A shock of hair had fallen over his forehead that gave him a dashing look. "I have wanted you since the first night we shared this bed."

"Good." Yet he didn't seem in a hurry to claim her. Instead, he threaded their fingers together, pressed her hands to the mattress on either side of her head. "I shall try to make your first time memorable."

Even in this he was concerned for her. She shifted her body, and as his shaft brushed along her sensitive flesh, she moaned. "Finish me, Brook. I only want you." Longing coursed through her, made stronger by his delay, and enhanced by anticipation. Forever after, she would finally know what it felt like to be desired by a man.

"Ah, Hope." He brushed his lips over hers. Then, with a powerful flex of his hips, he penetrated her in a long, smooth glide that didn't stop until he was fully sheathed. A pinprick of pain followed, and she squirmed, but the discomfort fled. His length filled her, stretched her, was snug into her as if he'd always been a piece of her that was missing.

"Merciful heavens, you feel wonderful." A sigh shuddered from her. Never in her life had she experienced anything like this. No one had told her how lovely lying with a man would be. Desperate for more of him, Hope canted her hips and took him deeper, and the sensation was so exquisite, another moan escaped. She clung to his fingers. "I cannot think…"

"Then don't. Just feel." Brook rested on his forearms as he stroked into her, slowly at first, the thrusts leisurely and tender, leaving no part of her body unclaimed. "You are gorgeous, inside and out, and I am beside myself with the gift you have given me."

Oh, he was romantic enough, and her heart shivered from his words, but she was too far gone to answer him. Pulling her hands from his, she looped her arms about his broad shoulders and clung to him in an effort to be closer still. Then she wrapped her legs about his waist and kissed whatever part of him she came into contact with as he increased his pace. Over and over, he pushed, harder and harder he moved as if he wished to join them permanently. Deeper and deeper came his strokes.

The rhythm was both calming and energizing. It was quite odd to try and describe, but each time he thrust, fractured shards of bliss streaked through her body. When Hope opened her eyes, it was to find Brook looking at her in wonder. She held his gaze, and for a moment he paused in the claiming of her. They communed without words or movement. Instead, their souls connected and something more precious than anything in the world was exchanged between them. It brought tears to her eyes, and then the moment passed, and he kissed her as if that would be the final time he would see her.

With each pass, the band of need stacking within her grew until she feared she would certainly break apart. A muffled cry left her throat and she wrapped her arms about him all the tighter while the duke's thrusting grew ever faster and more urgent.

"Brook!"

Release came upon her before she was ready, and it roared with veracity through her already primed system. Hope tumbled and pinwheeled through a field of white, sparkling light where all sound and thoughts were absent. There was only her and him, and it was the most glorious thing. Heated pleasure crashed over her, pulled her down beneath its waves, swept through her body until she bobbed along with it, powerless to resist, never wanting to come up for air. She drowned in it, succumbed to the vortex swirling within and for the second time that night, she fractured into a million pieces.

His chuckle chased the wave. Shortly after, the duke spent with a shout of her name she had no doubts their neighboring roommates would hear if they had retired for the night. Heat sank into her cheeks as his member pulsed. Seconds later, Brook collapsed on top of her. The comforting sound of his ragged breathing filled her ear, but it was the strength of his embrace as he wrapped her in his arms and turned them both onto their sides that helped guide her back to reality.

"This is, by far, the best Christmas I have ever passed." The whispered statement seemed overly loud for such a hushed and holy night, but she didn't care. She smiled when he chuckled and nuzzled the crook of her shoulder. Several minutes later, when her breathing returned to normal and the tremors faded, Hope snuggled deeper into his embrace. There were no regrets or worry to be had this night, for in this perfect moment, she was his.

I belong to him.

Her eyelids drooped with exhaustion as she glanced at the window. Big, fluffy snowflakes drifted by the glass, but it wasn't enough to further delay travel. With a yawn, she shivered from the cool temperature and burrowed beside the duke. In the distance, the sound of church bells rang, announcing the arrival of midnight and Christmas, but Hope merely rested her head on his chest, listened to his breathing, and let herself drift away. Tomorrow, he would find the notebook containing her unfinished manuscript tied with a red ribbon on top of the bureau. It was her Christmas gift to him, but right now, she was quite satisfied with what she'd already been given.

Tears would come later, for this was an aberration. Nothing more. He had never been hers to keep.

Chapter Fifteen

December 25, 1810
Christmas morning
Sometime before dawn

It was still dark as pitch when Brook woke. Gooseflesh covered his skin and shivers chased through his body, probably due to the fact he was completely nude and over the bedclothes instead of under. The pleasant ache in his muscles gave way to memories of last night where he'd indulged in too much rich food, too much brandy, too much dancing, and definitely too much scandal.

With one glance to his right, he grinned. Damn, it hadn't been a dream. *I am the most fortunate of men.* Her brown hair lay spread over the pillows, and one of her hands rested on his chest. Such delicate fingers, such soft skin!

Hope.

It seemed much like a dream, a scene straight out of his most erotic imaginings. He had coupled with Hope the night before, and it had been an amazing experience—a defining experience—and now it was Christmas. A time of new hope. He couldn't help the soft snicker. As quietly as he could, he left the bed and then covered her with the rumpled bedclothes. Poor thing would freeze to death, for they'd both fallen asleep shortly afterward.

When she murmured something unintelligible and rolled onto her side, he brushed a lock of hair from her face and let his fingers linger upon the curve of her cheek. While he watched her sleep, his mind flipped through the possibilities. Perhaps it was time to throw caution to the wind, take a chance, and grasp at love again.

Love.

Was he ready for such a big leap? After all, he'd barely pulled himself out of mourning and the ennui found following that. To say nothing of still missing his wife. Yet when he looked at Hope, each time he was in her company, as their eyes met, something inside him just... knew they had been meant to be together. Where he'd courted Deborah for months before finally achieving this particular feeling, after only a handful of days he'd found it with the woman sleeping in his bed.

Again, he trailed his fingertips across her cheek. She sighed and turned her head into his hand. Brook's chest tightened.

Faith.

He would need it to screw his courage to the sticking point. Was it madness to have reached such a conclusion and state in a handful of days? The way it happened was staggering, and she was as different as night was to day than his first wife, but it wasn't as terrifying as he'd thought. Brook frowned as he snagged a banyan from a wooden peg on the wall where Hope had hung it. She must have tidied the room yesterday afternoon. The silk was cool against his skin, and as he pulled the garment closed and tied the sash about his waist, again his regard landed on the woman sleeping in the bed.

So where did that leave him?

It didn't take long to ponder. A grin curved his lips. He was... happy, and he had been every moment in Hope's company, even when they'd shared grief and discussed their pasts. *I'm happy again.* Surprise circled through his system. That was something he hadn't achieved since Deborah's death, and he welcomed it back with open arms.

Padding to his traveling trunk, he kneeled, and then opened the lid. Good heavens, what now? Would Hope even have him? Would his elevated position in society frighten her away? What if she refused him on principal, for she was much younger than he? Rooting through his belongs for the handkerchiefs he'd gotten from the German princess, he paused in the search as another thought occurred to him. What the devil would he do with his aunt if Hope did agree to his suit?

It was something he would seek her counsel on, for a future duchess certainly couldn't become companion to a contrary peeress.

My future duchess. He rather liked the sound of that. She pushed him and challenged him, teased him and would no doubt take him to task if he did something she didn't agree with.

But that brought up more questions. The only things he knew about her were the parts of her history that had brought her grief, the loss of her parents, a bit of her time spent at her father's manor house. It tightened his chest with discomfort, for he'd known everything about Deborah by the time they'd wed, but perhaps there was more than one way to go through life with a woman. That was the purpose of a marriage, right? There were years ahead to learn each other's secrets.

The future. No longer did he look upon it with fear and loathing. All of a sudden, those years sparkled with new possibilities.

Stop woolgathering, Denton. You have a purpose this night.

Grabbing the small, flat box of handkerchiefs, he closed the trunk and then moved to the bureau. As he laid down the box, he saw the notebook waiting there with a red satin ribbon tied about it. A scrap of paper scrawled with his name had been placed beneath the ribbon.

What was this? He'd seen Hope write in the small, leatherbound notebook a time or two over the course of their stay at the inn, so it was odd that she would give him something so personal, but his pulse increased as he tugged on the ribbon and freed the notebook. The scrap of paper fluttered to the floor. The ribbon slipped to the top of the bureau. Too dark to read the writing inside the notebook, he quickly and quietly lit the candle waiting there, and then after checking to make certain Hope still slept, he bent closer to the flame in order to read the flowing, flowery handwriting.

The first page was loose and folded. When he smoothed it out, his name leapt in front of his vision, and he caught his breath.

My dearest Brook.

It is my wish that when you read through these pages, you will remember our time together at The Brown Hare Inn with fondness. It – and you – have certainly made an impression on me. I never expected to spend the holiday in such a lovely way, but then you came along and completely turned my head, convinced me to dream of things I have no right to think about. I don't know what will happen next, but perhaps a miracle will occur this Christmas and make those answers clear.

Until then, you have my respect and regard.

Hope

What did any of it mean? Was she referring to what she'd written on those pages or what was growing between them? Perhaps it didn't matter, and he was thinking too much on the issue. Not knowing, Brook read through the first few pages. Her style of writing was as bright and bubbly as she, and easily he became lost in the story. The hero in the tale happened to be a high-ranking and very respected duke. As of yet, he hadn't met the heroine of the story, but he hoped she had included herself within the fiction.

Suddenly, the need to be with her welled, so he laid down the notebook, blew out the candle flame, shed the banyan, and then returned to the bed. Once he'd burrowed beneath the bedclothes and gravitated toward the blessed warmth of her body, he sighed.

How had this change occurred in such a short span of time? Out of all the women in the world, why was he so fortunate as to stumble upon Hope, who was intended to become his aunt's companion? And now he couldn't imagine a day without her in it.

Well, Denton, you have certainly sent yourself tip over tail. What now?

Oh, why wouldn't the morning arrive faster? Excitement filled his chest, for he knew exactly what he wished to do in order to advance their relationship, but there was much to contemplate beforehand and a bit of planning to put into play.

"Brook?" The whispered inquiry seemed to dance upon the chilly air, but it was the sweetest sound he'd ever heard.

"Yes?" He slipped his arms about her and pulled her backside flush to his front. It was such a lovely feeling having her beside him in the dark.

"Are you well?" Hope lifted her head to glance into his face.

"I have never been better." How long had it been since he'd awakened in the night due to nothing more than anticipation?

"Is it morning already?" When she nestled closer into his embrace, rolled over to face him, his heart trembled, and warmth filled him.

"Not quite, but it *is* after midnight and theoretically Christmas Day."

"Oh." She took a deep breath. It eased out on a shuddering sigh. "Happy Christmas, Your Grace." Hope lifted a hand, cupped his nape, and then pressed a kiss to the underside of his jaw. "I am glad to spend it with you." The sleep-roughed tone of her voice, the fleeting touch of her hand, the heat of her body all worked at his undoing.

"Ah, sweeting, I feel the same." Then, because he couldn't have enough of her, Brook encouraged her onto her back, and he fit his lips to hers in the darkness. Awareness of her washed over him to harden his shaft. Would she object to a quick coupling to usher in this most holy of days, or would she embrace his enthusiasm with her own?

The darling woman came up to the mark spectacularly. She kissed him back with a hunger that fueled his. Her arms were around him, caressing, exploring, and everywhere she touched brought tiny fires that ramped his need.

Then he was entranced, spellbound perhaps, in her, on the idea of her, bobbing out to sea on the possibilities that he might have more feelings for her than he cared to admit to himself just now lest he was wrong.

Sighs and soft moans broke the silence, and when he thrust into her honeyed heat, Hope welcomed him with kisses and caresses and whispered words of encouragement. *Dear God*, it was all too easy — all too *right* — and for the first time in a very long while, there was a sense of belonging as he stroked into her.

She lifted her hips, met him for every push and penetration, and they indulged in a dance as old as time itself. Slowly, he claimed her, rocked gently against her body, communed with her soul, gave her everything that he was. Wanting to make her fly before he went, Brook urged her to bend her legs at the knee so that he might go deeper still. He played at her swollen pearl, tangled his tongue with hers, mimicked what he did to her in an effort to send her over that edge. Her body shook and tensed while faint fluttering contracted around his length. That first release was upon her.

All too soon, urgency tingled through him. His pulse pounded at his temples in time to the throbbing in his shaft. He kissed her, willed her to understand he wouldn't last. Hope was intuitive to his needs; she always was, and when she trailed a hand between them to rub a fingertip along the thin stretch of skin just behind his stones, his world tilted, shifted, spun out of control as a wave of pleasure swallowed him.

Never did he want to find his way back from being utterly, completely, unapologetically lost in her.

Twice more her thrust into the tight warmth of her, and when she shattered a second time, he went with her, falling down, down,

down into ecstasy. In the process, he was hurtled closer and closer into that secure state, connected with her on a level that had nothing to do with physical satiation and everything to do with belonging, with companionship, with love.

With a sigh of pure contentment, Brook rolled to his side and took her with him. The sound she made reminded him of a cat's purr, and he grinned into the darkness as she snuggled against his body. Damnation but this was all too lovely. Would it last? How could he be so certain when it might all be naught but an illusion brought on by their forced proximity together?

Believe, Brook.

He couldn't be sure, but the words infiltrated his passion-drugged brain, and they sounded as if Deborah had whispered them into his ear.

It's time.

For what? To move forward? To release his death-grip on the past, or at least loosen it? Odd, certainly, but then exhaustion was upon him, tugging at him to sleep while Hope's even breathing told him she was very nearly there as well. Putting his lips to the delicate shell of her ear, he said, "Wear the red gown tomorrow for Christmas." He wanted her to feel her best when he put his budding plans into motion.

A soft sound of protest escaped her. "Whyever for?"

224

"You shall find out tomorrow. I promise." Then he closed his eyes and let sleep have at him.

Once more, as per usual, Brook dreamed of Deborah, but this time there was a different feel to the familiar scene. Again, they were in his study. It had been a place where his wife had liked to relax, especially if he was busy looking over ledgers at his desk.

When he glanced across the room at her, instead of reading a book as was her wont, she stood at one of the windows, peering out with the sunlight turning her brown hair almost to burnished auburn.

"Are you well?" he asked, and with a frown, he noted her belly wasn't swollen with child. Where did this fall into his personal timeline if at all? There was no way to tell, for it was a dream and there was no conscious stream of thought here.

"Oh yes." Her grin was beautiful, almost angelic. "It is time, Denton." She had always called him by his title.

"For what?" It was the second time tonight she'd told him that.

"For you to find yourself in love again. To know what it feels like to belong to someone— body, heart, and soul."

"But... I still love you." His chest tightened, for the unknown loomed before him, and he didn't want to contemplate it if she wasn't there.

"Ah, dearest." As she drifted toward him, he rather doubted that her feet touched the floor. Was she a ghost, then? "You always will, and there is nothing wrong with that, for I will always remember you as well." When she reached out with a hand and brushed his face with her fingers, all he felt was a slight disturbance of air. "Please know there is capacity in your heart to give so much more love."

Was it possible to let go?

She laughed, but it was a faded sound of itself. "You worry but there is no need. I can see how you have changed."

"Meaning?"

"Simply put, you are happy. I have heard you laugh this past week, and it pleases me."

Gooseflesh popped on his skin. How much had the ghost of his dead wife seen? "Should I marry again?" It was the question sitting uppermost in his mind. Perhaps he wanted her blessing or at the very least her approval before he could make firm plans.

"You absolutely should, and I rather like the woman you have chosen." Though she smiled, her image was beginning to fade ever so slightly. "I think she will lead you on a merry chase, and that is what you need right now."

Though Brook silently agreed, he frowned. When he extended a hand to her, it merely went through the image of his wife. "Where will you be?"

Again, she glanced toward the window. "With our child. We had a daughter, Denton. Oh, you would have enjoyed meeting her, but for now, I shall look after her until we meet again in the world yet to come."

Sadness filled his chest, but the panic he'd become accustomed to never materialized. Instead, a new excitement had taken its place, but how could it when he was supposed to be missing Deborah? "I want to go with you."

"Not yet. It is not your time. You have many years of happiness ahead of you." When she met his gaze, approval shone in her eyes that were not quite as deeply brown as Hope's. "Love her, dearest. Love her with all of your heart. There is plenty of room. She is good for you and will make a fine duchess, perhaps in ways I never could."

As he talked, her image continued to fade. "Wait!"

"I cannot. Our daughter is calling. I must go." Deborah smiled at him. "Enjoy the remainder of your time on this mortal coil, dearest. The best years are ahead of you." Then her image went transparent, and the study around them dissolved as well. "Goodbye, my love. I am happy for you and wish you well."

Then, as he watched in astonishment, the house around him disappeared. In its place came the rolling fields of his estate in Hampfordshire with the manor house in the background. Snow lay on the ground, and the coolness of the wintertime air wafted over his skin. But then Hope was there, clad in her red Christmas gown with her hair loose and flowing, tied back with a red ribbon. She waved at him, ran toward him, and then she was there. He turned about with her in his arms. Their laughter rang on the air before he set her onto her feet and peered into her eyes. There was such welcome and love in those depths that his heart swelled, and he kissed those upturned lips.

Oh, but he wanted to grasp love into his life again. He wanted nothing more than to be a husband and perhaps try to fill a nursery once more.

Soon.

The dream faded but left behind sensations of warm contentment that he shifted in his sleep and pulled Hope's slumbering form closer to him in the bed.

Perhaps he *would* have her for a lifetime after all. Finally, he'd found the peace that had eluded him for the last two years, and he couldn't wait for the morrow.

Chapter Sixteen

December 25, 1810
Christmas afternoon

Hope hid a yawn behind the façade of sipping from her cup. A formal tea had been set up in the common room due to the holiday, complete with plenty of traditional sweets, savory hand pies and other wonderful edibles, and from the looks of it, the patrons of The Brown Hare Inn were heartily enjoying themselves.

Laughter and the low buzz of conversation filled the air. Coupled with the snap and crackle of the fire in the hearth and the scents of the holiday, it made for a lovely respite. High spirits were certainly the order of the day. Everyone was once more dressed in Christmas finery and seemed to be as happy and jolly as they were last night.

A secret smile curved her lips as she remembered what had happened after she and Brook had retired for the night. They had come together carnally after teasing each other throughout the week, and it had been the height of wonderful. Never had she imagined how much pleasure one person could experience during a coupling, but then the duke was quite talented. She had dreamed of him afterward, and at some point, he'd gotten out of the bed while it was still dark, but when he returned, they'd come together again in a quick bout of love making.

It had been no less lovely than the first, but he'd exhausted her beyond measure, so she'd stayed abed rather late today.

With another sip of tea, Hope glanced toward the windows where the sun was shining through the clinging clouds. The weather had taken a turn for the better, which was good, of course. According to one of the grooms, rain was expected tonight. It would help to melt some of the snow from the roads. Yes, they would be terribly muddy and rutted, but at least they would start to be passable perhaps in another handful of days.

A sigh escaped her. Knots of worry pulled in her belly as she continued to nibble on various tea cakes. Passable roads meant her time here at the inn was coming to an end. Confusion took hold, for though she wanted to get on with the trip and settle into her future in Yorkshire, there was a large part of her that never wanted to leave this little oasis. Largely, that was due to the duke's influence. His presence in her life had changed it irrevocably. Never would she forget him or what they'd shared.

Yet the practical side of her realized neither of them could linger. Their paths were not destined to permanently cross, and the thought had tears prickling the backs of her eyelids.

"You have the look of a woman wrapped in a quagmire of emotion," the magistrate said as he approached her table and then seated himself across from her. "Never say you are sad on this Christmas Day."

"I'm afraid I am, Mr. Pierce." She gently set her teacup in its saucer on the scarred and worn wooden tabletop. "My time here has been unexpected and lovely."

"Of course it has." Amusement sparkled in his hazel eyes. "You have had uninterrupted time with your husband. It was much like a honeymoon, if you will." The knowing expression on his face sent heat into her cheeks.

"Perhaps." They had certainly behaved as such.

"Where is the fortunate Mr. Gerard?"

"I couldn't say. When I woke, I saw him briefly. He gave me a set of dainty handkerchiefs as a gift then he left." She would treasure those bits of lawn and lace, just as she would the carnal memories they had made together. Yet he'd apparently remained busy enough that she hadn't seen him at all since the morning. After he'd thanked her for the gift of her notebook, he'd taken it and himself out of the room without explanation.

"Don't fret, Mrs. Gerard. I saw him out walking the grounds earlier, and from all accounts he seemed lost in deep thought. No doubt he'll turn up soon."

"I'm sure he will." But her doubts deepened. Now that he'd gotten what he wanted from her, after he'd taken her innocence, was he through? Was their association ended? Was that why he was outside? To check the condition of the road?

Tears welled in her eyes. Though she wanted to cry, Hope tamped the urge. She had to be strong. No matter how much she might wish it otherwise, her path and his would end once he escorted her to Yorkshire. He had his ducal life, and she was destined to be a companion. *I had hoped to tell him goodbye...*

From across the table, the magistrate made soothing sounds. "I didn't mean to upset you, Mrs. Gerard. Might I refresh your tea?" His hand was already on the teapot, so she nodded merely to let him think he offered comfort.

Then the door to the outside opened and Brook came into the common room. "Happy Christmas, everyone." With the greeting, he grinned to the room at large while casting a glance about the area. As his gaze alighted on her, that grin widened. "Just the woman I wanted to see."

Across from her, the magistrate chuckled. "Now there's a man who is on a mission. Seems he's brought a bit of excitement with him."

"How do you mean?" There was too much curiosity burning in her brain to remain quiet.

"Just look at how everyone in the room watches him and how he carries himself. Every woman wishes she was his wife, for he has heat in his eyes and only sees you. Each man in attendance is rotting with jealousy for the simple fact you have chosen him. Yet there is no doubt every person in this room respects him. They have no reason not to."

"Oh." Hope followed his movements with her eyes. When he removed his greatcoat, top hat, and gloves, he handed them off to a waiting footman. She frowned. Since when did he have the staff doing his bidding? The younger man gazed at the duke with near hero worship.

Brook crossed the room, fairly prowled over the floor in her direction. Oh, he was so handsome in the evening clothes he'd worn the night before, and… Her frown deepened. Where had he procured someone to cut his hair? Surely, he wouldn't have let one of the stable hands touch his golden locks, but someone had, for his tresses had been freshly washed, cut, and arranged into a popular style worthy of Beau Brummel himself.

"Goodness he is potent," she whispered, much to herself for she'd all but forgotten the magistrate sat at her table. Her mouth watered with the need to explore his form with her lips and tongue; seeing him in the sunlight with his broad shoulders highlighted and his lean, muscled thighs shown to perfection with those black breeches, impossible, naughty things flitted through her thoughts.

Every head turned as he went by. When he came close, the scent of sandalwood and citrus teased her nose. A hush fell over the room but why? At her table, he paused, greeted the magistrate but the bulk of his attention rested on her. "Hullo, Hope." A sheepish expression crossed his face. "I apologize for my absence."

"It is all right." Why were her words so breathless? This meeting was nowhere near as scandalous as what they'd indulged in. "What were you doing?"

"Reading."

"Outside?"

"Well, while having my hair cut. The stable master is quite talented with a pair of scissors." He shrugged as if all of that was obvious. He tugged her notebook from the interior pocket of his jacket. "I read every word you wrote in here."

"Oh?" Her hands shook so badly that she clasped them in her lap. "And?" Had he realized she'd written about him and her?

"You have much skill in writing prose. We need to nurture that." When he laid the notebook on the table, he caressed the leather with his fingers before training the whole of his attention on her. "How does the story end?"

"I..." Her throat was suddenly dry. "I hadn't thought that part out yet, but if you have an idea, I would enjoy hearing it." Would he know her words held two meanings? Did he want a continuance of what they'd had while at the inn?

"Perhaps I do." Mischief danced in his eyes, but before she could question him further, he turned away, apparently to address the room at large. "Over the past handful of days, everyone beneath this roof has known me as Mr. Gerard, a banker from London, and you have also known this lovely woman as Mrs. Gerard, my wife."

Murmurs of agreement went through the room, but the silence following was thick as everyone strained slightly forward, hanging on his every word.

"However, all of that has been a lie, one big work of fiction put forth to protect Hope's reputation and allow us to share a room, for there was only one when we arrived. I thought myself the lesser of the fates presented to her."

He glanced at her, but when she shook her head as her chest tightened with fear, he winked and turned away once more. "In reality, I am the Duke of Denton, and this is Miss Hope Atwater, and I'm afraid I have hopelessly and quite unrepentantly compromised her."

Merciful heavens! Why would he say that? The heat of embarrassment slapped at her cheeks as the magistrate stared at her in shock. As did twenty or so pairs of eyes in the room. A few gasps circled about, but the duke — damn his eyes — stood there with a slight grin curving his sensual lips.

"Let me explain." Brook held up a hand as if he prepared to orate on the floor of the House of Lords instead of addressing a room full of inn patrons. "If the snowstorm and the overly crowded inn hadn't have happened, I would never have been able to come to know this beautiful, wonderful, amazing woman who has completely turned my world upside down."

The urge to retch from the scrutiny climbed Hope's throat. She tugged on one of the tails of his jacket. "What are you doing?"

"Securing my future — *our* future." The intensity in his blue eyes had the power to strip the strength from her bones. When he kneeled on one knee at the side of her chair and took one of her hands, she gawked at him.

"I don't understand." Truly, she didn't, but an inkling of his intent wormed through her shock-ridden brain, and she gasped. "Surely, you aren't—"

"Oh, yes." Delight lay stamped across his dear face. "You see, over the course of our time together, I have come to admire and respect you. The counsel you give me, the gentle nudges into looking at a situation in different ways have made me think and examine the man I am… the man I wish to become."

"It was only regular conversation," she said in a soft voice.

"Gammon again." Brook squeezed her fingers. "I was a man trapped in grief with no way out to see the life that still remained ahead of him, but then you came along and changed my way of thinking even in that." His eyes bore into hers. "You shared your own stories of loss with me, and we bonded in that, came to a catharsis of sorts in that telling."

"None of that equates to the enormous on-dit you have given for the gossip mill just now."

"No, I suppose it doesn't, but I wished for our fellow travelers to have some background to understand this next part." With tears in his eyes, he tucked an escaped lock of her hair behind her ear with his free hand. "After some of the grief dissipated, I was able to see clearly, to be honest with myself about what I wanted in my life."

"Yes?" She couldn't dare to assume.

"It is you, Hope. You have come into my life, scrambled every bit of it up, and then when you put me back together, somehow pieces of you got tangled into pieces of me. I need you with me, now and always, for after thinking about little else for the past day, I am convinced you belong with me." As he peered into her face, he gave her the grin that sent hordes of butterflies through her lower belly. "After last night, I found peace for the first time in a long while, and that is why am I here now, kneeling before you, asking you this humble question." For long moments he held her gaze. "Will you marry me?"

Another round of gasps went through the room. The magistrate didn't even bother to hide the interest in his expression.

Oh, my. After thinking herself on the shelf and wildly unloved or wanted, a duke of the realm was now asking for her hand. "Are you mad?" She quickly pulled her hand from his then immediately missed his comforting warmth.

"Perhaps I am, but I did everything the proper way the last time around. Fate made certain that ended prematurely, so I thought to try things I bit differently this time."

Slowly, Hope shook her head. "You are merely doing this out of a misplaced sense of responsibility."

"Not so." Confusion shadowed his gaze. "I have never been more certain of anything."

"You wish to mitigate further scandal." But it was an excuse so she could marshal her own thoughts.

Wasn't it?

"Perhaps that is a tiny part of it—after all, I don't wish for my new duchess to battle the gossips once we return to London—I only speak the truth. My heart is very much being offered to you, sweeting. By choosing you, by loving you, I shall be guaranteed happiness until I am old and gray. Because I have hope." That quirky grin followed his attempt at humor.

Yet she couldn't believe he was serious. Then one of his words circled about her mind like ponies on a loop. "You cannot possibly *love* me."

"Oh, no?" His chuckle dispelled some of the mad tension building through the room. "Is not history full of miracles? Do we not believe in the very miracle that made this day's celebration possible?"

"Well, yes, I suppose that is true, but—"

"—no." Brook shook his head. Once more he took possession of her hand, and from the glint in his eye, he knew his argument had more strength. "With that line of reasoning, why can I not have fallen for you in a handful of days? The time we've spent together equates to a year's worth of meetings during a proper courtship, and sometimes a man just knows." When she remained quiet for her brain screamed at her not to fall for pretty words, he grinned. "Perhaps I should ask you this instead. How do *you* feel about *me*?"

Oh, dear Lord.

"I..." Heat grew in her cheeks as everyone in the common room stared at her with varying degrees of shock and pleasure. "I…"

"Yes?" One of the duke's eyebrows rose. The light of victory twinkled in his eyes.

Oh, he was insufferable when he was right! But he waited on a reply, and it was one she could no longer deny or hold inside. "I think I love you," she whispered as the magistrate chuckled. "But it is simply madness or perhaps wishful thinking."

"Is it, darling?"

The magistrate cleared his throat. "I rather side with your man, Mrs. Gerard. Any fool can see the two of you are besotted with each other."

"I…" Her breath came in quick pants while cheeks burned with both mortification and need.

Brook squeezed her fingers. There was no mistaking the love light dancing in his eyes. "I'm afraid I will need more of an answer than that."

Aggravating man. "I am perhaps falling in love with you." This time, there was no holding back her grin. "Yet it is quite impossible."

"Indeed, it is, unless you have hope, and sweeting, that is exactly what I want," he said in a whisper meant only for her ears. "In the event you haven't noticed, I am still on one knee, and that is rather unprecedented behavior for a duke, so will you dance with me in insanity? Please marry me, be my duchess." The heat of his hand holding her, the raw emotions reflected in his eyes, the earnestness of his inquiry all worked to break down her reserve. "We have a lifetime to discover every secret we both hold, for you have a great knack of ferreting out mine, and I look forward to the findings."

It was all so incredible. So beyond anything she could have ever dreamed for herself. No longer would she need to be a companion. A gasp escaped her. "What about your aunt?"

"She can continue the search for a companion, for my need of you is exponentially greater than hers." He dropped his voice and leaned slightly forward. "I can guarantee you will enjoy your time with me more than you will with her." Then he winked, and another piece of her heart flew into his keeping.

"You are serious." It wasn't a question.

"Absolutely. I love you. I need you, now and forever, in every way a man can. Take that chance. Don't you think you owe it to yourself to see how far you can go in this new direction?"

"I…" Suddenly, new possibilities opened ahead of her she'd never seen before.

The sound he made was that of a smug man who knew he'd won the argument. "I'll ask again. Hope Atwater, will you marry me?"

Excitement buzzed at the base of her spine. "You aren't just taking pity on me and saving me from scandal or the need to become a lady's companion?" She needed to make that clear. "I want there to be no regrets."

"There is no chance of it." Brook brought her hand to his lips and kissed the back of it. "What I feel for you is quite real." He put his lips to her ear, and added in a whisper, "I dreamed last night of Deborah, and for the first time, she urged me to let her go so I can move with you into the future, to be happy."

That was as good of an endorsement as she would ever have. "Oh, Brook!" Hope bolted out of her chair with a cry and threw herself into his arms. "Yes. Yes! I will be your wife, and while I fear I am dreadfully inadequate to be a duchess, I shall try hard to make you proud."

"Darling, can you not see I am that already?" With tears in his eyes, he removed his signet ring and then slipped it onto the fourth finger of her left hand. "It is a bit large, but this is only until I can take you home and find you a real ring from the Clevenger jewels."

"It is perfect and very much a statement of how this whole week has followed the insanity of invention."

"We will do great things together. I can feel it."

Once he stood and brought her up beside him, he kissed her quite soundly despite their audience. Hope didn't care. She looped her arms about his shoulders and kissed him back in an effort to show him how exactly she felt about him.

A round of clapping greeted them when he pulled away.

His grin could rival the sun outside. "Since the magistrate and a vicar are here, will you do me the honor of having a nuptial ceremony right now?"

"What?" Another round of shock went through her as she stared at him. "Here in this common room?"

"Yes." His grin widened and the corners of his eyes crinkled.

"Truly?" How was it possible this man continued to surprise her?

"Oh, yes."

"I hardly look the part of a bride."

"My dear, you are the very essence of a new bride, and that gown is quite stunning on you." He winked, and her knees wobbled. "Besides, I don't want to spend another day without you being my *real* wife, especially since I have compromised the hell out of you this week."

Heat slapped her cheeks. "Perhaps it was me who compromised you, Your Grace." Oh, she couldn't wait to marry this man!

"I am not about to dispute that fact."

Good natured laughter circled throughout the room. The German princess gasped and murmured about impropriety. A few of the servants in attendance smirked. But she didn't care. All of her worries had suddenly evaporated. "There is nothing I would rather do on this Christmas Day than marry you."

"If I may interject?" The magistrate rose to his feet with a frown as he looked at the duke. "You do not have the proper paperwork."

Vicar Bowling came forward, bouncing his gaze between them and the magistrate. "While I would like nothing but to perform the ceremony, Mr. Pierce is right. There are proper channels and rules. You will need a license."

The joy she felt plummeted into the pit of her belly. "Oh, no." She clutched at the duke's hand.

But she needn't have worried. Brook rose to the occasion with grace and elegance suited to his station. "What is the point of being a duke, Mr. Pierce, if one cannot manipulate a situation to his advantage?" He rested his gaze on the magistrate then on Vicar Bowling. "I am willing to make sizable donations to the church, as well as to the villages where you both reside if you would each grant me this concession today." Couched in his deep baritone, the words sounded entirely reasonable. "Once the roads are clear enough, I shall ride to the appropriate parish and apply for a license, for we both have been here long enough to provide residence."

For long moments, silence reigned in the common room, and once more, every eye was upon them.

Finally, the vicar spoke. "Well, since you and Miss Atwater have resided here at the inn for nigh onto a week, this is residence enough, I agree, and since I am the only member of the clergy here, I would say that is grounds enough for us to cobble together a license which will endure in these most remarkable of circumstances."

Hope glanced at the magistrate. "Do you agree, Mr. Pierce?" If he didn't, it truly didn't matter, for she had the promise that she would eventually marry the duke.

"I approve of the plan." He nodded, and Hope wilted with relief against Brook's side. "If anyone should cry foul, you send them my way, Your Grace. I will vouch for you." He sent his gaze about the room. "We all will." Then he grinned. "I know exactly what you feel for this woman and see what she feels for you. That is enough to convince me you are not taking further advantage."

"Oh, thank God." Brook clutched tightly at her hand. He smiled down into her face. "We are to be married. On Christmas Day."

Wild cheering filled the room. One of the guests called for rum punch. The innkeeper promised to bring out his fiddle for dancing.

Vicar Bowling smiled. "If you will allow me time to fetch my *Book of Common Prayer* from my room, we shall be underway in a twinkling."

"Of course." Once more, Brook brought her hand to his lips. "We are in no hurry."

Hope couldn't stop smiling. She fairly quivered with joy. "I am afraid of how happy I am feeling right now, and slightly in awe of you."

The duke chuckled, and the sound reverberated in her chest. "This is only the beginning, sweeting, but I know what you mean. If our hearts never felt anything, how would we ever know we're alive?"

"I cannot argue with that logic."

"Indeed." He put his lips to her ear and said just for her, "And tonight, I intend to show you how alive I am and how desperately I love you."

"Oh!" Heat once more sailed through her cheeks, but she didn't mind that either. "Every day that goes by, I love you more."

"Good, for if we are fortunate, we will enjoy years together." Then he swept her into his arms and kissed her again.

Sandra Sookoo

Epilogue

December 15, 1812
Clevenger House
London, England

Hope paused at the door to her husband's study, and with an index finger pressed to her upper lip, she paused and waited until the urge to cast up her accounts passed. Just like the last time she was increasing, the sickness came in the evening instead of the morning.

"Dearest, if I could have a moment of your time?"

The duke glanced up from the two ledgers he had open on his desktop. As soon as his gaze alighted on her, it softened, and he grinned. In the candlelight, the delicate skin at the corners of his eyes crinkled. "Of course." He scrambled to his feet and then ushered her to one of the low, leather sofas on the other side of the study. "Are you well? Is something wrong with John?"

The mention of their son's name made her smile. He had turned a year-old last month, and never had she been prouder of an accomplishment. "Calm yourself, Brook." She had never taken to calling him by his title. He would forever be Brook to her after the events at The Brown Hare Inn that had brought them together two years ago this month. When he seated himself beside her, she took his hand. "All is well, or it will be soon enough. For the moment, I am merely exhausted."

"Meaning what?" Concern creased his brow and shadowed his eyes.

"Patience." She patted his cheek. "Have you ever regretted the day you married me?" So much had happened since they'd met during that freak snowstorm, she could scarcely keep it all straight.

"Absolutely not. It was the best decision of my life." As he turned toward her, his knee brushed hers and tendrils of heat curled through her belly. "I have never loved you more."

"And you are pleased with our son?" Perhaps she needed the reassurance, but she did adore when he doted on her and their life together.

"He is a wonderful child who I suspect will be a brilliant wordsmith like his mother." The grin he gave her provoked one of her own. "Each time I see your first book sitting in a place of pride in our library, it immediately takes me back to that inn, when you found me and gave me back the sunshine."

Oh, he was such a romantic. Perhaps she shouldn't tease him overly much with this news. "Do you remember how we discovered I was carrying John?"

"Of course." He slowly nodded. "We attended a dinner party where Prinny was to make an appearance, and shortly before the fourth course arrived, you quietly vomited into a potted fern because you couldn't reach a ladies' retiring room soon enough." Then his eyes widened, and shock lined his face. "Are you...?"

"I think so. This feeling has all the same hallmarks." She twined their fingers together. "To be certain, I had the midwife in this afternoon. From what I can gather, and she confirms it, I am perhaps two and a half months along. The same sort of nausea is assailing me I struggled with when I was pregnant with John."

"You are increasing again." Wonder wove through the words. "A second child."

She nodded as tears filled her eyes. "Are you pleased?"

"Darling, I'm beside myself with happiness." The duke released her hand only long enough to hold her head between his palms and stare into her eyes. "Another baby. Never would I have thought I would have any of this..." His voice broke and he looked away. "You never fail to amaze me."

"Well, I didn't do this alone." In fact, ever since their marriage at that inn nearly two years ago, she hardly spent a day alone, and she couldn't have been more pleased with that fact. Her husband was an attentive and inventive lover, and they'd both decided to buck societal traditions by sleeping in the same bed. The only time she'd been apart from him in the duchess suite was shortly after she'd birthed their son.

"No, I don't suppose you did." The dreamy expression quickly turned into something more wicked. "Regardless, this is fantastic news. I cannot wait to meet this child."

"You will be a wonderful father to this babe just as you are to John." When a tear fell to her cheek, she wiped it away with a laugh. "If it is a girl, would you consider our family complete?" Their son resembled Brook, and secretly she wanted a girl that looked like her.

"I will be happy with whatever fate decides to give us." With a quick glance to the door, he slipped to his knees in front of her. Leaning forward, he pressed his lips to her belly through the fabric of her gown. "Hullo, little one. I am your papa."

Hope's heart trembled. "I am so glad I married you."

"So am I. You, my dear, are the reason for the wonderful life we both enjoy." Familiar need lined his face, and it awakened her own. "I shall wax poetic about that later. For right now, though, I'm going to show you how much I adore you, since you apparently don't believe me whenever I tell you."

"Brook!" Her squeal of mock-outrage only made him chuckle. "The butler will call us to dinner in half an hour."

Already, her husband had the silken skirts of her navy gown shoved up her legs so that it bunched at her waist. "Then he can wait." Gently but with firm insistence, he spread her thighs, opening her to his darkening gaze.

"You intend to leave the door ajar?" Though the staff was well-acquainted with their penchant for indulging in some sort of carnal play whenever the mood took them, Hope was always embarrassed those rare times they were caught in the act.

"Yes." He winked. "It adds a bit of heightened sensation, don't you think?" Then he buried his head between her legs, and as soon as he touched his lips to her sensitive flesh, she was lost.

Long ago, Hope stopped trying to bring a proper order to their lives. Each time she'd tried to talk to Brook about it, he said he'd had proper in his first marriage and that hadn't lasted. Now he wanted spontaneity and fun in the hopes it would give him a better outcome with fate. She couldn't fault him for his superstitions—and she did adore this wicked side of him—but she would teach their children to take that advice with a grain of salt.

Though life was fraught with obstacles and peppered with sadness at times, that didn't mean one needed to completely give up living altogether. The key to living a happy existence was remembering the past with a healthy dose of wisdom, enjoying the present by making good choices, and looking forward to the future knowing that fate might have other plans.

Having the person you loved beside you made the passing of the days more bearable— good or bad. And no matter what, never forget there was always hope.

The End

If you enjoyed this book, please leave a review on the site of your choice.

Regency-era romances by Sandra Sookoo

Willful Winterbournes series

Romancing Miss Quill
Pursuing Mr. Mattingly
Courting Lady Yeardly
Teasing Miss Atherby (coming February 2023)
Guarding the Widow Pellingham (coming May 2023)
Bedeviling Major Kenton (coming August 2023)
Charming Miss Standish (coming November 2023)

Singular Sensation series

One Little Indiscretion
One Secret Wish
One Tiny On Dit Later (coming January 2023)
One Accidental Night with an Improper Duke (coming April 2023)
One Scandalous Choice (coming July 2023)
One Thing Led to Another (coming October 2023)
One Suitor Too Many (coming January 2024)
One of a Kind (as part of the *Gentleman and Gloves* anthology
coming 2024)
One Track Mind (coming August 2024)
One Night in Covent Garden (coming October 2024)
One Christmas Disaster (coming December 2024)

Mary and Bright series

A Merry Little Crime Scene (a Mary and Bright mystery #1)
(coming December 2023)
An Intriguing Springtime Engagement (a Mary and Bright mystery
#2) (coming April 2024)
Autumn Means Marriage… and Murder (a Mary and Bright
mystery #2) (coming October 2024)

Diamonds of London series

My Dear Mr. Ridley (coming March 2023)
The Lady's Daring Gambit (coming June 2023)
Catch Her if You Can (coming September 2023)
Magic for Christmas (coming December 2023)
When the Duke Said Yes (coming February 2024)
Along Came Tess (coming June 2024)
A Ghostly Affair (coming September 2024)
Spending Christmas in Hell (coming November 2024)
The Duke's Accidental Mistress (coming January 2025)
Only Spring will Do (coming March 2025)
Not in His Usual Style (coming May 2025)
The Duchess Problem (coming July 2025)
The Recalcitrant Lady (coming September 2025)
A Bit of Christmas Fiction (coming November 2025)
If a Spinster Wishes (coming January 2026)

Hasting Sisters

The Devil's Game (coming March 2024)
A Second Summertime Courtship (coming May 2024)
An Impossible Match (coming July 2024)

Disreputable Dukes of Club Damnation

Ravenhurst's Return (coming November 2024)
His by Sunrise (coming February 2025)
Promised to the Worst Duke in England (coming April 2025)
The Devil's in the Details (coming June 2025)
The Duchess' Damning Letters (coming August 2025)
Buckthorne's Secret (coming October 2025)
A Duchess for Christmas (coming December 2025)
Pursuing the Duke of Hearts (coming February 2026)
In Hell by Default (coming April 2026)
To Woo a Duke (coming June 2026)
Three Nights with the Devil (coming August 2026)
To Hell with the Duchess (coming October 2026)

Colors of Scandal series

Dressed in White
Draped in Green
Trimmed in Blue
Wrapped in Red
Graced in Scarlet
Adorned in Violet
Embellished in Mauve
Clad in Midnight
Garbed in Purple
Resplendent in Ruby
Cloaked in Shadows
Decorated in Christmas
Tangled in Lavender
Persuasive in Pink
Disguised in Tartan
Attired in Highland Gold
Hopeful in Yellow
Imperfect in Peridot
Christmas in Crimson
Outrageous in Orchid (coming November 2023 as part of the *Earls and Pearls* anthology)

Storme Brothers series

The Soul of a Storme
The Heart of a Storme
The Look of a Storme
A Storme's Christmas Legacy
A Storme's First Noelle
The Sting of a Storme
The Touch of a Storme
The Fury of a Storme
Much Ado About a Storme (as part of the *Duke in Winter* anthology)

Author Bio

Sandra Sookoo is a *USA Today* bestselling author who firmly believes every person deserves acceptance and a happy ending. She's written for publication since 2008. Most days you can find her creating scandal and mischief in the Regency-era, serendipity and happenstance in the Victorian era, or historical romantic suspense complete with mystery and intrigue. Reading is a lot like eating chocolates—you can't just have one book. Good thing they don't have calories!

When she's not wearing out computer keyboards, Sandra spends time with her real-life Prince Charming in Central Indiana where she's been known to bake cookies and make moments count because the key to life is laughter. A Disney fan since the age of ten, when her soul gets bogged down and her imagination flags, a trip to Walt Disney World is in order. Nothing fuels her dreams more than the land of eternal happy endings, hope and love stories.

Stay in Touch

Sign up for Sandra's bi-monthly newsletter and you'll be given exclusive excerpts, cover reveals before the general public as well as opportunities to enter contests you won't find anywhere else.

Just send an email to sandrasookoo@yahoo.com with SUBSCRIBE in the subject line.

Or follow/friend her on social media:

Facebook: https://www.facebook.com/sandra.sookoo

Facebook Author Page:
https://www.facebook.com/sandrasookooauthor/

Pinterest: https://www.pinterest.com/sandrasookoo/

Instagram: https://www.instagram.com/sandrasookoo/

BookBub Page:
https://www.bookbub.com/authors/sandra-sookoo

Website: http://www.sandrasookoo.com

Also, if you want to join my ARC review team on BookSprout, here's the link:
https://booksprout.co/reviewer/team/10540/sandra-sookoos-review-team Bear in mind, these ARCS go fast, like in a few hours the day I post so make sure you're signed up for notifications.

Made in the USA
Middletown, DE
28 December 2022